AF425065

KING OF DEATH

JEWEL SHIPLEY

Copyright 2024 Jewel Shipley

All rights reserved. No portion of this book may be reproduced in any form without permission from the publisher, except as permitted by US copyright law.

This is a work of fiction. Names, characters, places, and incidents either are the product of the author's imagination or are used fictitiously. Any resemblance to actual persons, living or dead, events, or locales is entirely coincidental.

Tropes

Tropes: Possessive/jealous anti-hero, fated mates, he helps her heal, broken trust by a previous relationship, opposites attract

Acknowledgments

I would like to extend my sincerest thanks to Jennifer Julie Miller for her unwavering support and help. She has been a shining star in my journey as an author. I would like to thank my sister and alpha reader Luna Black for always being willing to talk books. A huge thank you to Amalee Keunemany for her excellent introspective feedback. My support system has made my dream a reality. I kindly and humbly thank you all.

This is for everyone who wasn't afraid of the boogeyman.

Editor – Partners In Crime Book Services: Lily Luchesi:
website: https://www.partnersincrimebooks.wixsite.com/authorservices
email: partnersincrimebooks@gmail.com
Cover Artist – RJ Creatives Graphic Services
Website: https://www.rjcreativesgraphicservices.com/
Email: rjcreatives.graphicservices21@gmail.com

Trigger Warning

Trigger Warnings

Please be aware that this book contains content some readers may find disturbing, such as mentions of a deceased spouse, domestic violence and abuse, graphic descriptions of violence, off page miscarriage, murder, gore, dubious consent, nonconsensual spanking, discipline, and excessive cursing.

Categories: Mythology, Dark Fantasy Horror, Women's Fantasy Romance

Chapter One

Marjory

Getting blood out of clothes was such a pain in the ass and she had just bought these shoes to wear for the Valentine's Day party next weekend! Who knew killing your piece of shit husband could be so messy? Marjory Hempstead looked down at herself in dismay. Her clothes were liberally soaked in blood, and was that a small piece of flesh hanging off her shirt cuff? Upon closer inspection, she discovered it was part of one of his fingers. She didn't remember cutting off one of his fingers… Oh well. She plucked it off her shirt and tossed it in the hole.

Marjory sighed as she took a break from digging and leaned against the shovel she found in her garden shed. She needed to make sure the hole was deep enough that no one would know his body was buried under the roses that were intended to be used as a cover for his early grave. How fortunate Jeff had *insisted* they purchase fully mature plants instead of small starter bushes. The three bushes were completely leafed out and covered in blooms, not that the blooms would last long after being transplanted. Roses were notoriously difficult to maintain. Zinnia, while colorful and easy to maintain, was not *sophisticated* enough for hosting. Maybe Jeff's rotting corpse would feed the finicky fucking plants and help them flourish. Wouldn't that be lovely? And she could always add more flowers to the area if need be.

It was the dead of night. Well, actually it was a bit after midnight if you wanted to be precise, which Jeff was always precise as she glared at what was left of him. Thank the good Lord Jeff had insisted on the ten-foot privacy fence instead of the usual eight-foot and the extra-large lot in this godforsaken HOA he had forced her to move into during the fifth year of their marriage. Not that he had asked her if she wanted to move into the monstrosity of a house in a fucking HOA, of all things. It felt good to cuss. She hadn't been allowed to behave with any less than full decorum, and she was sick and tired of it. Being a trophy wife was not all it was cracked up to be.

Marjory sighed as she resumed digging. Her mind drifted to the events that lead to her current activity. She and Jeff had gone to the gynecologist/fertility specialist appointment earlier today. The one that Jeff had scheduled for her because of the miscarriage she had on their "romantic and exotic" vacation to the Bahamas. Only Jeff would schedule that kind of appointment on a Friday afternoon, expecting good news so he could go home and give his wife a celebratory fucking. The fact that he tracked her fertility cycle and knew she was supposed to be ovulating this weekend added insult to injury. What a joke. It wasn't the least bit romantic for your manipulative, controlling, abusive husband to beat you so severely that you miscarried.

All due to a simple slip of the lip at supper. If she hadn't drunk that second glass of champagne, none of this may have happened, but she did, and it had. The specialist had told them that because of the severity of the miscarriage and the resulting complications caused by Jeff refusing to take her to the emergency room, not that anyone knew he had refused her medical care, until all the bruising had faded, she could no longer have children. The shock had rendered her speechless and struck terror deep within her.

She knew that her value to Jeff had drastically diminished. Pretty only went so far without being useful. The main reason he had married her was because she was exceptionally beautiful yet meek, malleable and had no one. That she would have been even easier to control with a child in the house was just a bonus point, as far as Jeff was concerned. He'd also needed someone to inherit his business when he was ready to retire. That he would have preferred a son was a given. The child she had so briefly was on the cusp of being far enough along to find out the sex, but, sadly, she hadn't made it quite that far.

The ride home was held in silence, as Jeff had been so furious he couldn't speak. After arriving back at the house and entering into the kitchen from the connecting garage, Jeff had grabbed her by the arm and spun her around to face him. "You're fucking useless to me now! The fact that you were nice to look at, a good lay and so easily trained to please me, along with a womb that functioned, were the only things you are good for! You sniveling, worthless bitch!" he sneered. The fist to her jaw was not unexpected, but the bloom of pain that sparked behind her eyes and pooled in her belly was a shock. No matter how many times he hit, the pain never became something she got used to. Jeff had allowed her to drop to the floor and kicked her in the belly as he went to walk past her. She landed in the space between the island bar and the kitchen counter, so she was hidden as soon as he had ascended halfway up the staircase.

Marjory wasn't sure what prompted her to look around the kitchen in desperation instead of being the meek creature he had called her. She hadn't ever fought back before, but this time she knew he was going to kill her if she didn't. Marjory had realized in that moment, she wasn't ready to die. That there were things that she still wanted to do before she left this earthly plane. Her gaze landed on the handle of a kitchen knife; the handle was barely visible on the island counter above her. It was the boning knife she used earlier to prep supper with.

Jeff's disappearance out of the kitchen wasn't a surprise, and she knew what he went to get. He liked to inflict pain and got off on it whilst doing so. Fucking sadist. She had never enjoyed the mockery that was her married sex life. He was fetching his "toy box." She knew he was going to *play* with her one last time, just because he could, in order to exert his power and control over her, and then she was going to die a slow, painful and drawn-out death.

She had managed to reach up and grasp the knife in her hands as she heard Jeff returning. The knife was secure in her possession as he came around the corner from the living room into the kitchen. She felt, rather than saw, him reach for her neck to drag her up off the ground, and Marjory knew that this would be her sole chance. As he pulled her up, she slammed the knife concealed in the curve of her body into his stomach with every ounce of strength she had.

The funny thing, Marjory mused as she contemplated her actions, was that he didn't make any noise the first time she stabbed him. The sound he made was more of a gasp, as if the shock rendered him speechless or the force of the blade had robbed him of breath. The second time had caused him to squawk, the sound a chicken makes when you grab it unexpectedly, but it had been a muted sound, as if the evil had already been oozing out of him along with the blood splattering onto her pristine tile floor. After the first and second time she stabbed him, she sort of lost count of how many times she used the knife on him. Enough that he was almost unrecognizable by the time she recovered her senses.

Marjory shook her head to clear it as she tucked a strand of her icy, white blonde hair back behind her ear that had fallen out of her carefully styled bump during the kitchen altercation. Snooki from *Jersey Shore* had nothing on her as far as hair bumps went.

She needed to focus on what she was doing and her surroundings. She would have time to gleefully reminisce later. After inspecting the hole she dug, Marjory decided it was deep enough. The handle on the shovel was roughly four feet long, and the top of the hole was about six inches above that. The fact that it had taken her hours of digging attested to her determination.

Marjory slowly climbed up the ladder, mindful of the soreness in her abdomen, she had put in the hole as it became deeper. It wouldn't do to get stuck in the damn hole before she could shove Jeff into it. After successfully climbing out of the hole, she crawled on her hands and knees until she was on the other side of Jeff's body and began to push. She should have wrapped him in a shower curtain. It would have been less icky if she had. The feeling of her hands sinking *into* his body with a wet squelching sound was almost more than her stomach could take. No wonder they always used plastic or the proverbial shower curtain in movies. It was much less mess. Her husband had not been a small man by any means, and his dead weight was proving to be difficult.

Heh, dead weight. How punny, she thought, with no small amount of sadistic glee. Marjory was mildly concerned that she was losing her mind, but that was something to deal with later. With one last shove, she rolled Jeff off into the hole, pausing a moment to enjoy the fruits of her labor. Groaning, she picked herself up, putting her hands to the small of her back to rub the stiffness out, then began the arduous task of filling the hole in.

When she had the hole partially filled, she reached for the first of the three rose bushes and strategically placed it so the other two would be equidistant from each other. Details mattered, especially when it came to her precious garden. It was the only thing she had that was hers and that she enjoyed. It was quite literally her pride and joy. Well, that and reading, but Jeff had only allowed her to read books that he approved of, not anything she truly loved.

After she finished planting the roses, thoroughly watering them, and applying a heavy layer of compost, she stepped back to observe her work. The roses looked beautiful as well as tasteful, and since they were in the backyard, the HOA couldn't say a fucking word about them.

Marjory walked over to her cute, picturesque garden shed and put her shovel and gloves away, then turned to go inside. As she walked in the back door, her nose wrinkled at the metallic scent of blood emanating from the state-of-the-art kitchen, however she was simply too tired and in too much pain to clean that particular mess up. It would have to wait until tomorrow, she thought with a sigh as she padded up the stairs, wondering how she could google 'how to get blood-stains out of tile' without it being suspicious. She pondered how she was going to explain Jeff's absence after this week-end, as he was expected back at work Monday morning.

Marjory stopped in the doorway of their…no HER bedroom. She looked around the room, seeing it with the perspective of a widow, not a wife. There was very little to the room. A large dresser was against the wall that led into the opulent bathroom. The bed was on the adjacent wall situated between the doorways leading to his and hers walk-in closets.

Matching nightstands flanked the head of the bed on either side of the headboard, the wood a rich dark oak that coordinated with both dressers. A dainty, feminine antique vanity and chair were placed on the wall across from the bed. She had been expected to prepare herself for each day there. The same wall also had the door entering the room attached to it. The four-poster bed dominated the windowless sterile space and had been a place of pain, degradation, and horror for years. The fact that the master bedroom lacked windows was a major selling point for Jeff when he'd initially toured the house. The room was done in cool shades of silver and blue, nothing bold, no jewel tones. It was boring, plain and simple. Jeff had not allowed her to decorate the bedroom with any of the seasonal or holiday décor he demanded the rest of the house be covered in. The areas of the house that other people might see were to be decorated like something you would see in a magazine. Since it was February, the rest of the house looked like she had vomited pink hearts everywhere, even if it was tastefully done. Sleeping all alone in the king-sized bed was going to be wonderful, she thought to herself as she slowly changed into her pajamas and laid down on the pillow top mattress with a sigh of relief.

Chapter Two

Vyllon

He didn't know his beautiful, broken little bunny had it in her as he watched with prismatic eyes as she rolled the body into the hole she had to have painstakingly dug. The stiffness of her curvaceous body told him more than he was sure she would ever willingly admit to. He was most displeased that she had to take care of this particular task by herself. He would have been happy to do it for her so that her dainty, little hands never had to sully themselves with the likes of that piece of shit mortal currently beginning the putrefaction process. Taking the life and soul of the defiler would have granted him extreme pleasure, especially knowing that the souls he chose to destroy would never reach the gilded roads above or the fiery depths below and would not have the chance at reincarnation. Not that souls banished to the underworld had much of a chance to begin with. It was still a hope for those trapped in the realm of damnation. The souls he consumed were as if they had never been. He was not a soul harvester or a guide for those that had passed; he was the ultimate punishment for mortals and immortals alike. The legendary boogeyman, so to speak. He cursed in frustration as he observed her filling in the hole; the moonlight reflecting off her platinum-colored hair. He wanted to go assist her, wanted to order her to go inside and rest, but he had not yet property introduced himself. His introduction into her life would have to be handled with care, as one could not make a second first impression. His little bunny had suffered. Her aura was ripe with it, the colors muted where they should be blindingly bright. Vyllon noted that even though the colors were dull, they had not changed since the last time he had beheld her. They were still a swirling mixture of white, silver and gold. The shadowed overlay did not penetrate her aura, it merely enshrouded it. Proving that her suffering hadn't corrupted her soul.

He may be a danger to all, but he was not a danger to *her.* She would be the sole being on the face of this planet and all the planes of existence that would be safe from his.... appetites. He may be an evil motherfucker, but not even he abused the truly innocent. It was easy to tell who was truly innocent by the color of their auras. Poor decisions always left a mark. Literally. There were rules against harming the true innocents of the worlds that not even he was bold enough to break. Those that did had to answer to him. He was the final judge and executioner. He enjoyed his existence and preferred not to have to deal with messy things like repercussions. The weight of time had eroded what little conscience he had possessed as a young being, yet he was held by ancient rites to do no harm to those who had not earned his wrath in some manner. The seriousness of the offense was to be determined by him and dependent upon the being he was dealing with, the offense could, and oftentimes was, slight.

He wasn't sure if his little bunny remembered who, or exactly what, had held her as her body had rebelled against the abuse it suffered, causing her to lose her child. He had morphed his corporeal form to something similar to human, enough that, in her pain ridden delirium, she had not noticed. In fact, she had clung to his form with maddened desperation, crying out to the cosmos, to any being or deity that would listen to save her unborn child. Due to his presence, her pleas had not been heard. Those that listened for the despair of mortals would not heed a being in *his* grasp and for all his power, he did not have the ability to save a life. He was death.

The hours that slowly passed, then and now, were of little importance. He was eternal; thus, he would wait for her to finish her task. He knew that this was something she needed to do. His interference would only be a hindrance and cause her more angst. So, he waited. Time meant nothing and everything to him.

When she finally entered the dwelling, her gait slow and shuffling, he assured himself that she was inside and safe before approaching where the defiler lay. He waited until all the lights in the house had been doused and then drifted across the open expanse of the well-manicured yard to the freshly laid flowerbed. The touch of his little bunny was everywhere as he felt his chest swell with pride to learn that she was so talented with living things. He was a creature of death. The fact that his mate embodied life would balance him well. His current form was not corporeal, but he did not want to cause her any undue stress, not at the current time, anyway. He thought with a smirk. She needed to become comfortable with him before he rewarded her impending devotion with the pleasure; he knew she had long been denied. If he had lips, he was sure they would be stretched in a facsimile of a smile.

Upon reaching the freshly planted roses, he focused on the defiler's brain. He needed information, but the brain needed to be relatively fresh for him to extract it. His essence slid into the space where consciousness had once dwelled. Perfect. He was not so dead that information could not be extracted. If the brain was damaged or the body had been dead for too long, he would not have been able to acquire anything. He began siphoning what he needed from the defiler. Had he done this on a living person, it would have reduced the phys-ical body to a husk as he was removing what made a person a free-willed, thinking being. What a shame that the defiler was already dead and he could not feed on the man's terror and horror over what was happening to him. As he would have let this one remain conscious of the horrors being inflicted upon him. He was not a kind being, and the defiler had touched what was *his*. That no one was aware that *she* belonged to him was of little importance. This transgression was not to be permitted.

As he siphoned from the corpse below, his non-corporeal body began to solidify, taking on the form of the being he stole from. This was not ideal as this form was one his little bunny had no liking for, but it was necessary so that he could infiltrate her life without the rest of the mortals being aware. He was a vain creature, so he did make a few modifications along the way as the form took shape.

He had waited so long, so very long for her. Dreamed of what she might look like and had longed for her sweet embrace as he walked from eon to eon. He couldn't wait for his little bunny to wake up in his arms. For that's what a good mate does. He holds her, ensuring nothing disturbs her slumber.

Chapter Three

Marjory

Marjory was having the best wet dream of her life as she hummed in pleasure and allowed her body to sink further into the plush bedding. She had not felt natural desire in longer than she wanted to focus on, but batted that line of thought away with a slight frown and focused on her desire, allowing the feeling to sweep through her body and mind. It felt good to luxuriate in her sexuality. Her full, lush breast was plumped with tightened nipples and her cunt was dripping wet with need. She let out a lurid moan, basking in the sensations rippling through her body.

She felt her dream lover's hands drift over her body; the slight rasp of his fingers tingled as they made their way to her aching breast. Marjory didn't question why she was topless since she had gone to bed fully clothed; this was a dream after all. She reached up to grasp the headboard. After all the bullshit she's put up with, her dream lover could do all the work. She was just going to lie there and enjoy herself.

She was not prepared for the pinch when it came. The contrast of the pinch to the light teasing strokes upon her breast shocked her and drove her ardor higher. It should have woken her up. Her body had never reacted naturally with pleasure when pain was applied to her person. Jeff had tried for years with a combination of aphrodisiac drugs and mental manipulation training to force her to crave pain and to only become aroused when he hurt her. This pinch, however, was a stark contrast to the merciless touches she had endured. This pinch had not truly hurt. It was a brief sting that licked her pleasure with dark flames.

She couldn't discern any pattern, so she never expected the small, stinging sensation from the hands alternating between lightly rolling her nipples and sharp pinches. It was a tease more than anything else. A hint of what she was in store for. Marjory huffed in frustration. This was her dream. Dammit, she deserved to cum. As if sensing her rising ire, her dream lover ceased tormenting her nipples and went to remove her pajamas. Marjory felt the silk sleep shorts whisper down her legs, the smooth texture tantalizingly added to her mounting pleasure.

Her shorts disposed of, the hands returned to her thighs, urging her to spread them as warm breath caressed her pussy.

The first touch came as a long lick from her ass to clit. The texture of the tongue was rougher than she was accustomed to, but it was a decadent sensation in its abrasiveness. The tongue began long, slow strokes on her clit, almost methodical in nature, as if the tongue had never done this before and was learning as it went, attuning itself to her to see what caused the strongest reaction. Each lick was precise and deliberate, making the throbbing deep inside her worse, forcing her body to climb higher and higher. Marjory allowed her hands to drift from the headboard and into the hair of her dream lover. She used her hold on his head to direct him where she wanted his attention most.

Palms brush caresses over her thighs, moving around her hips to grasp her ass in a firm grip. The tongue abandoned her aching clit and descended to the well of her pussy, seeking out the sweetness at its source. Marjory gasped as the tongue entered her in one swift motion. The sensation was unfamiliar, but not unpleasant. She hadn't ever been tongue fucked before and her imagination was working full force on how she would like it to happen. Tapered at the tip, the appendage within her thickened towards the base, causing it to stretch the opening of her pussy deliciously.

A muffled groan drifted from between her thighs, the sound caused Marjory to pause for a moment but the tongue inside her redoubled its efforts, flicking against her g-spot mercilessly, almost as if it was trying to distract her as a light, massaging touch was applied to her clit. The simultaneous sensations of having her clit and g-spot stimulated caused the pressure in her lower abdomen to rapidly build as her orgasm was wrenched from her almost brutally. The pleasure burst across her body like fireworks lighting up the night sky as the tongue within and continued to lash at her, forcing a second earth-shattering orgasm on her. The hands on her ass tightened and shoved her deeper into the mouth that was guttling her pussy. It surely had to be a dream, as no human could open their jaws like this. She could feel the edge of sharper than normal teeth on her mound and ass cheeks. It was as if the first and second orgasms were just a taste and now that her dream lover had gotten that first taste; he was desperate for a deeper draught from her willing body. That was fine with her. Her body was begging for more pleasure.

Marjory felt something begin to press into her ass. The slick she had leaked from her pussy had slid down and eased the way for thick fingers to penetrate her with ease. The combination of sensations caused her to come a third time, the orgasm catching her by surprise as she rarely had one orgasm, let alone three in one session. Her body trembled with the force of her completion, the tongue slowing its ministrations in increments, allowing her body to come down easily but not withdrawing from her body. It was as if the tongue was soothing her and praising her pussy at the same time. Marjory signed in sublime satisfaction.

As her consciousness woke, she slowly became aware of the feeling of something solid in her hands, felt the texture of hair between her fingers…but that didn't make any sense she was dreaming and was all alone. She had made sure that she would be alone and free for the rest of her life.

Marjory cracked open her icy blue eyes, looked down and screamed in sheer horror.

Chapter Four

Marjory

Marjory gaped at the sight before her, disgust and horror warring within her for supremacy. She was unsure which would win out as she felt her mouth begin to water with the precursor of vomiting. The feel of her slick mixing with the saliva from whatever the fuck had just been tonguing her was making her stomach roll. The desire to retch was building low in her belly. Jeff, or at least something that *looked* like Jeff, was kneeling between her wantonly spread legs. The tongue that had so recently been pleasurably embedded inside her was slowly returning to the mouth it belonged to. The length of the tongue, not to mention the texture, was not natural and not something her husband had ever possessed. At first glance, if one did not look too close, this thing would pass as Jeff. A friend or acquaintance would not have been able to tell the difference, but every facet of Jeff's appearance and being had been imprinted on her brain after the years she had been forced to spend with him. Its mouth was just a bit too wide, the teeth slightly too sharp, and the eyes shone with a light that had never graced her husband's countenance. That this thing made the façade of her husband slightly more menacing was not something she wanted to think about.

Terror rendered her immobile and speechless. Her flight or fight response was broken. After years of abuse, any fight had been beaten out of her and running had never helped her with Jeff, so her body was frozen in place, as if her body was encased in cement. She was not sure what she should do, what she should say, or even what to think.

The.... thing in front of her sighed in exasperation. "There is no need for you to fear me, little bunny. I mean you, specifically you, no harm, and the scent of your disgust is bordering on insulting. I know you achieved pleasure, more than once, and it tasted delicious upon my tongue. Alas, I have been remiss and rather, shall we say, forward? Allow me to introduce myself. I am Vyllon, at your service." The Not-Jeff had slid off the bed to stand beside it and offered her a courtly bow as he spoke. It was as if he was a courtier from the Dark Ages. Though his voice sounded like Jeff's, his words and the inflection in which they were spoken were, most assuredly, NOT-JEFF.

As the shock wore off, a deep well of anger began to take its place. Her fear was taking a backseat as well. If his word was to be trusted, he wasn't going to hurt her. He had ample opportunity to do her harm and chose to pleasure her instead. Why did the universe hate her so much? What had she ever done to deserve all this bullshit? Her shock and fear slowly faded. No sooner did she finally rid herself of Jeff, only to find this Not-Jeff in her bed and taking liberties with her body WITHOUT HER CONSENT. She was sick and tired of being used. That he did not take any pleasure for himself was not something she'd had time to contemplate. It was the violation of her person, yet a-fucking-gain, that she was sick and fucking tired of.

A dark chuckle lured her mind back to the matter at hand and the Not-Jeff standing beside the bed, waiting somewhat patiently for her to acknowledge him. The fact that he was naked was not something she wanted to focus on. She didn't let her eyes fall from his for a second.

"How dare you! What gives you the right to touch me? To take liberties with my body? Have you ever heard of this thing called CONSENT?" she sneered as she yanked the sheets up from the foot of the bed to cover her vulnerable, shaking, naked body. Not that she had anything he hadn't already made himself intimately familiar with, much to her dismay and chagrin. That she could still feel her pussy pulsating with aftershocks did nothing but stoke her temper hotter.

Without warning, his arm snapped forward and wrapped his hand around her fragile throat, his calloused thumb gently caressing the smooth skin along her jaw. She could feel the faint prick of nails where his fingers wrapped around her neck. The action had been so swift she hadn't even had time to flinch. "Because, little bunny, I have been waiting for you since the dawn of creation, and now that I have you, you are mine and no one will tell me that I cannot have you. Not even you," he whispered darkly to her as he loomed over her.

The sudden cacophony of the doorbell blasted up the stairs, interrupting what she was sure would have been additional information to freak her the fuck out.

Chapter Five

Vyllon

It was a shame that he could not eat the annoying mortal that had interrupted him and his mate. His mate had very few genuine friends and the one impatiently waiting on the front step was one of them. The defiler had made it clear that he hated Amalee and had done everything in his considerable mortal power to get her to leave the company of his little bunny. That he was unsuccessful was apparent. He admired the female's fortitude in refusing to be cowed away from her friend.

If he was to stay here for any length of time, and he fully intended to stay wherever she was, that infernal ringing thing would have to be removed. His sensitive ears were still ringing from the screeching emitted from the infernal device located in the foyer. Although it was amusing to watch her attempt to scramble into clothing without releasing her grip upon the duvet cover. Speaking of coverings, he reached for the garments he had retrieved from the defiler's closet prior to waking his lovely mate with his tongue. It would be best if he dressed in the defiler's clothes until he convinced his little bunny to go elsewhere with him. At least the defiler had good taste in clothing. He recognized all the brands being rather expensive and the texture of the materials was of higher quality. The trousers were a bit snug around the thighs as he tucked his modified cock into them. He smirked; the real Jeff had what was called a micropenis, if he recalled the term correctly. Vyllon had taken great joy in allowing his real cock to stretch out into this vessel. He was permitted to make modifications to vessels during the initial absorption and after that, he was relegated to the specifications of that particular vessel. He could become any vessel he chose once the absorption was complete. He could access the former beings' forms and memories. Refocusing on his task, Vyllon dressed quickly as he watched his mate dart frantically around the room after she had disappeared into the bathroom, slamming the door shut to perform her morning ablutions in private.

Having finally donned a matching set of frilly underthings, a pair of figure curving, high-waisted blue jeans and a black flowy blouse, he watched his mate hurry to the door only to come to an abrupt stop. "Oh, no! The kitchen! I didn't clean it last night!" she wailed in panicked horror as she collapsed against the doorframe. "What am I going to do? I didn't think Amalee was going to get here this early! She never gets here early?? We always eat lunch later rather than earlier because she runs behind! I can't believe I slept so late! Why fuck is she early the one day I don't need her to be early? Then there is the whole whatever the fuck you are thing! I still have your spit leaking out of me, for crying out loud! Bitch better have brought Pad Thai with her...." she ended on a weak uttered murmur.

Vyllon paused, his humor getting the best of him, even if he was slightly disgruntled at still being called a "thing", as he made his way to her deliciously crestfallen figure. She hadn't made it past the bedroom threshold before her panic had flayed her with ragged edges like a cat-o'-nine-tails flayed flesh from bone. He felt her body stiffen as she tried to lean away from him when he gathered her into his arms. He barely refrained from rolling his eyes. She was not as attached to him as he was to her.... yet. It would behoove him not to make his exasperation with her reticence obvious. "You need not worry, little bunny. I took care of the kitchen. It is as if nothing ever happened. Take some deep breaths to compose yourself before you descend the stairs to let your friend in," he soothed.

Her delectable little face frowned up at him in skeptical disbelief. "There's no way you could have possibly cleaned that entire mess up.... it would have taken you hours, and you would should still be cleaning on it as we speak if you wanted it squeaky clean"

"Ah, you are still operating under the assumption that I am human and confined to things such as human limitation. I am not human, nor am I limited to what a human can do. Removing all traces of the defiler was simple. I merely absorbed what was left of him into my being. His agony made his blood taste all that much better." He ended with a haughty smirk.

Some, not all, of the leery tension eased from her frame. The relief causing her body to sag against him for a brief moment before she straightened again, pulling away from him with a weak smile. She had allowed her body language to soften, only slightly, towards him. It was not much, but he would take whatever he could get from her, no matter how small a concession.

"I suppose I owe you a thank you for that…. not that you're going to get one! I'm still fucking pissed off at you for touching me without permission. We are also going to have to discuss that truly *awful nickname* you've decided to label me with!" she ended with a huff.

"As you wish…little one," he mildly acquiesced, quirking Jeffs' eyebrow in a manner the real Jeff had never managed.

Chapter Six

Marjory

When Marjory went to open the front door, Not-Jeff intercepted her. No, not Not-Jeff. The thing had a name. Vyllon. The fact that it was so close to the word villain did not fill her with comfort. His palm gently laid over her hand as he made her pause prior to opening the door.

"I think it would be wise to keep the fact that I am not who I appear to be to ourselves. I can sense how much regard you have for the female on the other side of the door and would hate to have to kill her," Vyllon murmured with a sardonic smile. Marjory stilled and felt her entire body go cold as ice. She did not know this being that wore Jeff's face and had no clue if he was joking or being serious. His words sounded like a dire threat, but the tone in which he had delivered them was almost teasing. Marjory wasn't sure which one to believe. The words or the intonation. He did not just threaten the only friend she had in the entire world…. did he?

The sole human being that cared if she was happy, sad or even alive. Marjory was fuming, and the bastard had the audacity to smile at her in a patronizing and placating manner. So, he had been joking! As if what he said made perfect sense and she was the one that was taking his words out of context. Other worldly being or not, he had to go, and he needed to go sooner rather than later. She refused to trade one tyrant for another. Her freedom hadn't even lasted a full day! Marjory chose to overlook the creature for his ignorance. Surely, he was not up to date on human customs and mannerisms. Considering the courtly bow he had given her earlier, she figured his information was a few hundred years old.

Marjory brushed him aside and opened the door to her friend's scowling face. Well, at least that remained the same. Amalee would come to see her but did not enjoy having to put up with Jeff. "I'm sorry to keep you waiting! I slept in this morning." Marjory greeted with a sunny smile.

Amalee's frown deepened as she took in her friend with dark brown eyes full of intelligence. She knew what usually happened when Marjory "slept in." It was because of either taking a beating or trying to recover from Jeff's twisted version of the marriage bed. She sneered in Vyllon's direction as she took in the faint bruising on Marjory's jaw, as Marjory had not had time to cover everything up with makeup.

Marjory felt her face heat with embarrassment that she had been so frazzled she forgot to put concealer on.

"Sorry I'm early. You can fuck off Jeff. You're not wanted for girl time, as per usual." Amalee addressed Vyllon with a sneer as she flicked her should length black hair back out of her face with an impatient hand as she moved past Vyllon into the foyer. Her boldness was attributed to the fact that Amalee had a family that would not tolerate anything happening to her, a fact that the real Jeff had been aware of and it had infuriated him to not be able to retaliate against a person he deemed beneath him. Marjory felt a stab of guilt. The being Amalee was addressing was not the reason she was bruised and stiff. He had many things to atone for, but hurting her was not something he was guilty of and the fact that she was unable to make the distinction bothered her. Marjory was not one to place blame for specific actions on those who did not deserve it. Vyllon had seen the expression on her face and shook his head in a barely perceptible movement. Amalee missed the short wordless conversation as she was adjusting the bags she was carrying as she walked.

Amalee followed them into the kitchen. Trailing behind Marjory and Vyllon as she muttered under her breath about shithead husbands that needed to take a hint and that she didn't slave over her stove for fucking Jeff, because Amalee had in fact brought food with her. It wasn't Pad Thai, but it smelled delicious and if Amalee had made it, it would be delicious. In another instance, Marjory would have found her friend's bated comments amusing as she normally did. Amalee didn't suffer fools lightly, and she had been trying to convince her for years to kill Jeff. Joke was on her. Marjory finally did the deed but wasn't sure how to tell her friend.

Marjory's anxiety was skyrocketing the closer they got to the kitchen. He said he had cleaned it by absorbing everything into himself, but what if he missed something? Her gazed darted rapidly around the kitchen as they entered, looking for any scrap of evidence that Vyllon may have missed. Seeing a pristine kitchen soothed Marjory's ragged nerves. He must have seen something in her face to indicate her relief. He angled himself so Amalee couldn't see his mouth as he leaned in to speak. "I told you that I cleaned every trace of what happened last evening up. You have nothing to fear." He murmured to her. Marjory was sure he meant to sound soothing, but he came across rather condescending. She really didn't need this shit. He had pricked her temper twice in an hour, a temper she thought had literally been beaten out of her. She was sick and tired of superior, condescending men.

Amalee moved around them with a scoff, eyeballing the tender display with disdain as she set the bag full of food down on the counter next to the sink. That's when Marjory's eyes landed on the boning knife that was lying on the kitchen island. Her body was between the island and Vyllon, so he did not see her notice the knife. His focus was on the delicious aroma wafting across the kitchen. How fortuitous that he had left it where she had tossed it. With a mind full of self-right-eous anger, she grabbed the knife, almost without conscious thought, pivoted to face the body next to her and stabbed Vyllon as hard as she could.

Chapter Seven

Marjory

The soft snick of a knife sliding through flesh was loud in the quiet of the kitchen. Amalee had turned just as Marjory stabbed Vyllon in the chest. "Holy fucking shit Marjory?!? What did you just do??" Amalee shouted in alarm; her body frozen in disbelief.

Marjory didn't move and didn't take her eyes off Vyllon. She was staring in horror at what she had just done. A swift intake of air was the only indication Vyllon had felt anything at all as the knife pierced where his heart should be. Marjory wasn't sure what made Vyllon, but it would have killed a human man.

Vyllon reached up and grabbed the thick handle of the knife, removing it with a wet squelching sound. The viscous fluid that began to flow from the wound was not bright red blood. It was an oozing black ichor that showed he was definitely not human. Amalee made a sound that bordered between a snicker and a mild amount of alarm. "Well, that's definitely not human. Who the fuck are you and where the fuck is the real Jeff, because you are totally NOT JEFF."

Vyllon heaved a heavy sigh. "Darling, had I known you were in the mood for additional flirtation, I would have kept you in bed longer. The invitation you just issued will have to wait until we are alone. I do not think you would approve of me bending you over and fucking you in front of your friend." The voice that emitted from Jeff's countenance was not Jeffs. This was a deep booming bass that rattled out of a human shaped chest. The depth of sound that emitted was not something a mere human could pull off. Marjory's eyes flicked down to his groin area briefly, just long enough to confirm that yes, he was in fact aroused by her fucking stabbing him! That did not bode well if he found her attempt at murdering him to be a form of flirtation that caused him to achieve an impressive erection…. that was decidedly bigger than anything her husband had ever possessed.

Jeff's body began vibrated as Vyllon groaned in frustration. "I wish you had not of done that little one. I will have to shift forms in order to seal the wound. You are not yet ready to see my true corporeal form. It will only make you fear me more, but I do not possess the ability to seal the vessel I am currently wearing, as it is just a vessel and not my true self." Jeff's form wavered like trying to look through water when the wind ripples it. The skin went from white with an olive undertone to pitch black as the sound of bones popping filled the room as the body stretched and contorted from that of a human man of above average height to a monstrosity that had to reach at least seven feet tall. Clothes ripped and fell in tatters to the ground as the body within in them exceeded the limitation of the cloth. The horns that erupted from his skull within the hairline and positioned behind either temple were just like Maleficent portrayed by Angelina Jolie in the Disney movie added at least another foot to his height as his horns came within inches of touching the eight and a half foot ceiling. Limbs lengthened as well, his arms became longer and proportional to his new height. Marjory noticed that his hands had an extra digit on them. Instead of the normal five one would find on a human, his hands boasted six digits; five fingers and a thumb, to be exact. His lower limbs snapped as the ankle joints bent backwards like a dog would and the feet got shorted and became more like a paw where the weight is distributed on the toe. As her eyes traveled back up his body, Marjory noticed movement behind him and found that a tail had sprouted from the base of his spine; it was long and sinuous, with a blunt end that looked textured. She noticed that he did not have external genitalia. There was a slit where his penis should have been.

His face became more angular, the cheek bones sharp and jutting as his eyes sunk within the skull and the forehead protruded. The facial structure was bestial and primitive, like the Neanderthals of ancient Europe. His nose was flat and almost muzzle like, not protruding off the face at all and his mouth was far wider than a human though his bottom lip was full, the top lip was thin and almost a mere slash of flesh. During his shift, the wound on his chest had sealed completely and the black ichor it had been leaking disappeared, as if it had never been. The transformation couldn't have taken more than thirty seconds, but it felt like time had slowed to a crawl as Marjory watched what was unfolding in front of her.

A massive black hand landed on the island next to Marjory's much smaller human hand, not quite touching her, as he leaned in. "Hello, little one." Vyllon rumbled gently as he leaned down to look into her eyes with his own that reflected all the colors of a prism.

Amalee, who had been strangely quiet throughout the transformation, walked over in front of Vyllon and stuck out her hand. "I don't know who or what the fuck you are, but you're not Jeff, so that makes you better already. I'm Amalee, Marjory's bests bitch. It's nice to meet you…" she trailed off and looked up at him expectantly.

Vyllon didn't show any signs of shock at the introduction. He extended his right hand and shook hers gently. "I am Vyllon. It is nice to meet the one who befriended my mate and offered her respite from the defiler." He intoned respectfully as sharp white teeth flashed within his mouth as he spoke.

Throughout this introduction Vyllon had not taken his eyes off Marjory as he waited for her to react to his new form. Marjory was still in shock. This is what had eaten her out this morning so well she had come three times!

Seeing that her friend was in a state of shock, Amalee moved to the kitchen cabinets and began to withdraw plates. She set the plates on the island and retrieved cutlery from the drawer next to the stove. "Marjory! Snap out of whatever shit you have going on right now. We are going to sit, eat and have what I am sure is going to be an exceptionally informative conversation. You look like you are about to fall over, so you need food. Food is always the answer or carbs are always the answer. Either way, we are going to sit and eat like civilized beings." Amalee bossed. She then looked over at Vyllon. "I think you are freaking her out more, looking like that. Can you switch back to Jeff?" she asked tetchily.

Vyllon smirked. "Yes, it will take but a moment."

Chapter Eight

Vyllon

Vyllon had changed back into the vessel of the defiler and retreated upstairs to redress himself as Amalee had set the kitchen table with three place setting and put the food in the middle upon the artfully designed table runner. His mate was giving him a wide berth. Her aura indicated she was extremely unsettled as the colors were tumultuous, writhing about her as her emotions were inside. He could scent her anxiety just like he had scented her rage right before she had stabbed him.

Vyllon smiled to himself as he sat at the head of the table. He was more than a little aroused at the display of pique she had expressed as he discreetly adjusted himself. The fire in her eyes had been delicious to observe. The bite of pain as the blade pierced him was nothing more to him than the warmth that would soon bloom across her ass as he disciplined her for, in her mind, trying to kill him. He never said he was a sane being, but his mate would not be allowed to think that she could kill him. It would be sometime before he admitted that the only beings that could end his existence were the archangels, demigods or gods. He admitted that his little mate would have to work out the negativity that had permeated her being because of the experiences she had been subjected to. Vyllon was sure she would try to get rid of him at least once more, but that did not bode well for the health of their future relationship if he did not allow her to act out now. He wanted to worship her and for her to be devoted to him. He would not subject her to the same type of hell she had experienced with the defiler. Her punishment would allow her to express her regret for her actions in a manner that would not harm her but would also allow her to submit to him as the dominant partner, and he would relish being the one to deliver said punishment.

She didn't know it, but allowing herself to feel anger instead of shoving it back down inside proved that she was healing. Her spirit was not as broken as she thought. If it was, she would not have fought back when her husband planned on killing her. She would not of so delightfully reprimanded him for whatever slight she had perceived against her earlier.

He watched as Amalee, and his mate moved to seat themselves at the kitchen table. Amalee, apparently experiencing little to no fear of him, sat to his left without hesitation. His mate, however, hesitated between the seat next to Amalee on her left, which would place Amalee between them, or the seat directly to his right before finally deciding to sit in the chair to his right.

It made his heart warm that she had decided to sit to his right. Long ago, in another time and place, sitting to his right was a place of great honor. That was when he had his own court as the infamous King of Death, but that had been millennia ago and was of no consequence anymore. He had accepted what had happened and had moved on. Dwelling on it would do him no good. He smiled over at his mate, allowing the warmth he felt for her to show on his borrowed face. He was sure it was an expression the defiler had never shown her with any truth behind it. She paused as she went to take a bite of food and peered at him with a hesitant smile. She still hadn't directly addressed him after he had changed forms.

"Now that we have gotten comfortable, ask your questions. I can see that you are both buzzing with them," he offered with a begrudging smile. It wasn't technically against the rules for him to disclose his existence to mortals, but it was to be done with great caution, ere he had to quiet them, sometimes permanently.

"Obviously, you aren't human and you are definitely not Jeff Hempstead, so who and what are you?" Amalee asked with barely restrained curiosity.

"As I have already stated, my name is Vyllon. I am what

you would refer to as 'the boogeyman' or more specifically a *bogyan*. I am the creature that goes bump in the night. The ultimate punishment for those who wrong the innocent. The beings that are so foul, even the depths of the underworld do not want them answer to me. I was created before man achieved enlightenment and self-awareness. I have lost track of the millennia I have seen and after a while, the counting loses its luster," he explained. "Humans are just one of the beings that I hold accountable to the golden rule of 'thou shalt do no evil.' There are many pantheons of gods, just as there is the one God that Christians worship. The one God is rather new and has not been around as long as some of the older pantheons. The old gods created a vast variety of beings, in their collective images, just as the one God made man in his. I am not the only boogeyman, but I am the first that was created. The old gods saw the beings they created as their children and would not hold them accountable for their actions, which lead to wars between the pantheons. I, and my brethren were created to make sure all beings, no matter their creators, were held accountable for their actions." He leaned back in his chair as he observed the two women as they took in what he had just said. It was quite a bit for a mortal to wrap their minds around, and he would allow them the time to process the information. Very few mortals in today's world even acknowledged that the old gods had existed out of what they labeled mythology.

"What am I to you?" Marjory asked with softly spoken hesitance after a moment.

"You are the sole being that was created to be my mate. You are the light to my darkness and the other half of my blackened soul. You, I am sure, will also be my conscious. If I ever possessed one, it has been eroded by the passage of time because of the filth that I encounter daily."

"Oh..."

Chapter Nine

Vyllon

The rest of the meal passed with the two females sitting in quiet contemplation. He did not blame them, as he had divulged a large amount of information, some of what was contradictory to what they had been taught regarding mythology as well as religion.

Marjory had been the first to rise from the table and began collecting plates and cutlery to take to the kitchen sink. He had observed as the women worked in tandem to clean the remains of their midday meal, their movements spoke of familiarity as they chatted about the party that was scheduled for the following week's end. It had piqued his curiosity as soon as they had mentioned it. He would enjoy taking his little bunny to a party themed for lovers.

That had been several hours ago, and his mate had

retreated into her garden after Amalee left. She had been studiously avoiding him. He had enjoyed watching her ignore him as he sat on the back porch under the awning. He was a creature of darkness and preferred not to sit in the direct sunlight. It wouldn't harm him; he just didn't care for it.

"You cannot ignore me forever," he called to her from his seat. The afternoon had waned as evening approached. The shadows beginning to lengthen as the sun made its slow descent across the horizon.

Her attention had been on the brightly colored blooms in front of her, attributed to the mild winters of this part of the world, but paused as his voice reached her. He heard her soft sigh as she sat back on her heels and turned her head to face him. "Honestly...I have no clue what to say to you," she replied. "I was finally *free*, and then you showed up and ruined it. I do not need or want another domineering, controlling, and manipulative man in my life." She ended on a sneer, her lip curling in disgust.

It made his heart heavy that she resented him so. He had waited so long, but her resentment was to be expected. She had been ill used and what he was about to do next would only make her resent him more. Until she repented, then she would not be released from the negativity shadowing her aura. Vyllon would relish being the one to assist her in that journey. He rose from the chair and walked towards her with a slow, steady stride. He extended a hand to her, waiting for her to decide if she wanted to touch him and accept his offer to help her rise from the ground. After a brief hesitation, she placed her delicate hand within his and he gently assisted her up.

"I cannot understand exactly how you feel, as I have never been in a situation like you were with the defiler. What I can tell you is that you are my mate, and I have been waiting for you longer than you can fathom. I will be patient, but I will not leave. There is nothing on this planet that can make me leave you now that I have finally found you. I do not care if you like me because I will make you love me. You will never be mistreated by me, but I will brook no disobedience from you, such as your actions earlier in the kitchen. All actions have consequences and it is my utmost pleasure as your mate to show you the err of your ways and correct your disobedient behavior."

His poor little mate's body had gotten tighter and stiffer the more he had talked as he led her back across the yard and into the house. The sound the French doors made as they walked into the kitchen made her flinch. All the color had slowly drained out of her face and her current pallor was that of a corpse. He had seen what the defiler did to her during her "training" sessions and was sure she was thinking she had traded one jailer for another. Had, in fact, basically said the same thing aloud several times. She would soon realize that he could correct her without damaging her. There would be pain, but only the kind of pain that exacerbates pleasure.

She balked as they approached the stairs, turning away from them in a feeble attempt to escape as a whimper emitted from her throat. The scent of her terror was a pungent cloud surrounding her body. Vyllon scooped her up into his arms as one would carry a bride across the threshold, only he carried her up the stairs and into the master bedroom.

He fully intended to replace all the horror filled memories she had of this room with pleasure. Even if there was a bite of pain accompanying that pleasure, it would still be titillating for his little bunny. *He would make sure of it,* he thought to himself as he gently laid her across the bed. Her beauty struck him as she lay there like a sacrifice. She was a sacrifice. His sacrifice for all the toil and evil he had seen; she was his just reward.

He merely needed to convince her of it.

Chapter Ten

Marjory

Marjory could barely breathe as he gently laid her across the bed. The fact that he still looked like Jeff was only adding to her terror. She had been so abused by her husband she was willing to beg Vyllon to change forms before he did…whatever it was that he was going to do to her. She didn't think her brain could handle being abused by the image of her dead husband. "Please, please don't look like *him*. I'll beg you if that's what you need," she whispered brokenly, her voice catching on a sob.

"There, there, little one. You need not beg for that. You will beg me for many things, but not that," he replied as his form began to waiver. Having witnessed him change forms twice earlier in the day took some of the shock out of the action. His eyes never left hers as he shed Jeff's guise. The eyes changing from Jeff's pale brown to glowing embers that accepted no true color. He shook, similar to how a dog would shake off water, as he finished shifting.

"You may disrobe by yourself and submit to your punishment or I will rend them from you as part of your punishment. It is your choice," he rumbled, his voice full of dominance as he loomed over her prone figure on the bed.

"I'll take them off. Please don't tear them. I like this blouse and finding jeans that fit me is difficult. I would prefer them in one piece," she acquiesced. He had leaned forward and put one of his overly large hands on either side of her body, essentially caging her in. Marjory began trying to get undressed while she laid on her back on the bed, she supposed that he was making it more difficult on purpose but wasn't sure his intent. After finally wiggling out of her clothes, she laid bare before him, her chest heaving because of the level of exertion she had to put forth to get her jeans over the curve of her ample ass.

Vyllon peered down at her as if he was savoring every piece of her body as it had been revealed. Once she was naked, he reached one hand to the nape of her neck and drew her up into a sitting position, causing her nipples to lightly brush his chest. The brief contact sent a zing of sensation through her nipples and down to her pussy. His skin wasn't skin at all. It was a hide of tiny, fine hairs so dense it was textured like velvet. He noticed her nipples as they began to bead into hard points and smirked down at her. "You will find that I am *nothing* like you are accustomed to."

Vyllon maneuvered her body like a rag doll as he sat on the edge of the bed and draped her across his lap, allowing her elbows and knees to rest on either side of him as her head was bowed forward, resting it on the duvet cover. Her previous experiences had taught her to keep her body loose and relaxed so it could be manipulated with ease, which had always resulted in less pain for her. Even though her mind railed at what was happening, her conditioning kept her body malleable.

Once he had her body positioned the way he wanted, the sound of Vyllon's deep voice pulled her out of her mental musings. "For attempting to kill me earlier today, failing to apologize for it and for being ungrateful of the pleasure I gifted to you this morning, you have earned your first punishment," he explained as his right hand roamed across the surface of her ass in featherlight soothing touches. His left hand appeared against the nape of her neck, pinning her in place. She felt movement around both of her ankles as they were lashed together with something warm and sinuous in its movements, the only explanation being his tail as both hands were currently occupied elsewhere. She was thoroughly pinned and held in place, but the manner in which he had arranged her was comfortable. Her comfort was not something that had ever been a priority before and the difference was something she noted immediately.

The rhythm of his hand began to change as soothing caresses turned into soft pats, as if he was warming the area up for what was to come. The first slap, when it came, caught her by surprise and caused her ass to clench with the shock of it. Marjory forced herself to relax, remembering her hard-earned education in matters such as these.

He began gradually, allowing her body time to acclimate to what he was doing to it. Each smack was delivered in a different place at random, so the same exact spot was not hit twice in a row. The burn built in increments, catching her by surprise with its intensity when it became a hot sensation of pain each time his broad hand landed against her soft ass. Marjory had sworn to herself that she wouldn't say a word, wouldn't object and wouldn't apologize to him, but the blows continued to rain down upon her without mercy. As if he was aware of her inner thoughts, he angled his hands to catch the bottom curve where her ass met her thigh and began to alternate between there and the fleshiest part of her ass. When that didn't elicit the response he wanted, he added the backs of her thighs to his range as well and applied a harsher strike to her sensitive skin. He rained blows across her ass and thighs without mercy until, finally, she could take no more. "I'm sorry! Please make it stop!" she wailed. Her ass and thighs were on fire and the pain was so bad she almost couldn't stand it. The skin had become so sensitive that each blow felt worse than the last. The heat emanating from her skin was a fiery conflagration that burned its way through her entire body, not just the areas he had focused his attention on.

"What exactly are you sorry for, my soft, sweet, delicious little bunny," Vyllon crooned darkly to her, never halting his hand as he spoke. He was larger and far stronger than Jeff ever had been. Her feeble attempts to get off his lap didn't work and only caused him to smack her harder for trying to escape her punishment.

Marjory was almost mindless by this time. Not even Jeff had ever punished her this long! "I'm sorry for st-st-stabbing you and for tr-tr-trying to ki-ki-kill you! I'm sorry I didn't ap-ap-apologize to you for it and I'm sorry I didn't th-th-thank you for pleasuring me this mo-mo-morning!" she wailed, each word catching on a sob as she cried out, tears streaming from her eyes as they rolled down her cheeks onto the duvet cover, she had buried her face into.

She felt his tail relinquish its hold on her ankles as it gently trailed up her legs to tease the burning hot skin on her thighs. He used his superior strength to lift and turn her body until her ass was pressed against the cradle of his hips, forcing her painfully abraded skin to brush against the sinful texture of his pelt. He placed each of her legs on top of his, ensuring the backs of her thighs rubbed against him agonizingly as his hands cupped her heavy breast, pinching her nipples to the point of pain. The position forced her legs to be spread far apart, as he was so much broader. It was then that Marjory realized her pussy was wet and her clit was desperately throbbing. She was far wetter than she ever had been when Jeff had punished her with a spanking, but then he had always used some sort of tool. He hadn't ever used his hands and Vyllon's hands were rough in a way Jeff's hadn't ever been. At some point, the pain had pushed past something in her brain, a block she had put there to keep herself sane while Jeff had been played with her. Vyllon had maintained her punishment until she was forced to acknowledge him and what he demanded of her.

Marjory's entire body jolted at the first touch of the textured end of his tail on her clit. She was so primed it wouldn't take much for her to climax. "Tell me, do you deserve to cum?" Vyllon asked, his voice contemplative. "Naughty mates that have earned a punishment don't deserve to cum…but I find that I am selfish male and wish to see you fall apart on my lap while my tail fucks you." Before the word 'lap' had fallen from his mouth, his tail brutally entered her in one thrust and he delivered a light slap to her clit. All the sizzling heat that had built during her spanking spiraled together in a hot, electric jolt, culminating in the hardest orgasm Marjory had ever had. Every nerve in her body sung as ecstasy poured into her entire body, as his ribbed tail brutally pumped against her g-spot without mercy, prolonging her orgasm and forcing her higher and higher until she screamed with the sheer intensity of it. The last thing Marjory remembered was the feel of muscular arms catching her as her body sagged and her mind drifted out of consciousness.

Chapter Eleven

Vyllon

His little bunny had given him a wide berth after waking in his arms the morning after her punishment. She had been quiet and somewhat withdrawn as she went about her daily task. Vyllon was sure that she needed the time to become accustomed to his presence in her life and the fact that he was not going to leave. Ever. He wasn't an unreasonable being, but he would not allow her the slightest bit of hope that he would leave her alone. In all honesty, he was probably going to be a stage five clinger, as the youth of this century call that level of neediness.

Vyllon had spent most of the day in the elaborately decorated living room reclined on the sumptuous sectional leather couch reading. The décor in the entire house was rather bland for his personal taste. During his wanderings, he had discovered the door across from the master bedroom led to a well-stocked library; the room was full of books. Three of the walls had shelves built into them and were full of books. The fourth wall contained a massive window overlooking the backyard, with a padded bench seat tucked into the alcove. The room was also full of tropical plant species that would not survive the current cold weather outside. They were tucked throughout the room in an elegant manner that added to the ambiance of the room. A heavy antique wooden desk with a comfortable looking ornate chair behind it sat in the middle of the room with the front facing the door. He was sure she situated it that way, so she was never caught unaware should the door be opened quietly.

It was clear that his bunny was the one who had stocked the library, as it was full of literature a female would covet. There were entire sections devoted to specific subjects such as gardening, interior design, history, classic literature and how to books. When he had come across the children's books, it made his withered heart ache. He was unsure if his little bunny's body was capable of carrying another child and wouldn't know until she decided to finalize their mating bond. He had forced himself not to linger by the brightly colored text and moved away from them with regret and longing filling his chest with a heavy weight. It was quite by accident that he had discovered the romance novels and how he had enjoyed how clever his mate was. He was sure the defiler would have frowned upon Marjory reading such material, so she had hidden it by changing the exterior covers. The book he was currently engrossed in was about extraterrestrials with breeding kinks, but the cover stated it was a comprehensive gardening dictionary. How very clever of his little bunny to acquire what she wanted and figure out how to hide it right under the nose of her jailor.

His cock had begun to thicken as he read further in to the story. His own selfish desires of breeding his little mate caused a physical reaction so strong it had caught him by surprise. His attention was drawn from the arousing text as the object of his desire calmly walked into the room and moved around the furniture to stand in front of him, the coffee table the only obstacle between their bodies. Her body language was not antagonistic, nor was it timid. Vyllon closed the book and set it on the glass-topped end table next to the couch and noticed how she blanched then blushed upon noticing what had held his attention while she ignored him throughout the day. It would be interesting to see if she addressed his reading choices. She took a deep breath and studiously ignored the book, choosing instead to focus on whatever had made her seek him out. Vyllon gave her his undivided attention, noticing that it made her hands tremble ever so slightly. Her remedy was to clasp them together in front of her to still them.

"I want you to take me on a date."

Vyllon leaned forward, resting his elbows on his knees as he gazed at her intently, waiting for her to finish as he was sure that was not the sum total of all she had been thinking about all day. "Since you have forced your way into my life, and don't appear to be willing to leave. It seems I'm stuck with you for however long that may be. I deserve to be wined and dined. Not just have some otherworldly being arbitrarily stating that I belong to him and expects me to go along with it. I killed the last man that treated me like an object instead of a person. I will not go through that again. I assure you; I learned my lesson about trying to kill you and I won't try again, but what I can tell you is that I will not love you. I will not turn to you for anything with free will. I will refuse anything and everything you offer me if you do not put forth the effort to know me," she ended passionately as she took a step back, unsure of what his reaction would be to her ultimatum. Normally, Vyllon was not one to take ultimatums with any vitriol. However, this was his mate and nothing she had said came as a surprise. Part of her punishment the night before was breaking through the walls she had built around herself because of the defiler's cruel treatment of her. It was also to show her baser self that she was safe with him, even in the midst of being punished for her transgression. Her conscious mind may not have acknowledged that, but her subconscious has as evidenced by her confronting him now. It made him quite proud of her. She was right to demand the things she had spoken and it would be his greatest pleasure to seduce her, woo her and ultimately make her fall in love with him.

"I would be happy to take you on a date. I do not disagree

with any of your statements. I want a mate, not a servant, and not a slave. I will do whatever it is you want of me, except leave. That I will not do. Anything else within my considerable power is at you demand," he intoned gravely. "A Sunday evening out of the house sounds quite nice. Where would you like to go?"

Chapter Twelve

Marjory

Marjory smiled to herself as she got ready for her date. The reflection in her vanity mirror showed a woman that had a sparkle in her eye and joy illuminating her face. She couldn't remember the last time she had been so happy. To say that Vyllon had been taking her seriously was an understatement. He had thrown himself in to planning at least one outing a day per her demand that he court her. She had to admit, if only to herself, that he was beginning to make a dent in her emotional armor. It was hard to remain impervious to him when he was going out of his way to cater to her every whim. To further prove that he listened to her, Vyllon shed Jeff's countenance before he entered the bedroom each evening. It had taken some time before she had admitted that the spanking he had given her had been a direct result of her own foolish actions, and that she had earned her punishment by trying to murder him. Vyllon had not drawn the line at merely taking her out on dates. He had taken over most of the domestic chores in the house as well. Marjory had not had a break from housework in more years than she wanted to admit to. She wasn't sure who or what he had acquired all of his knowledge from but it was comprehensive. She had woken up to breakfast in bed every morning this week, only to come downstairs to find that the kitchen was spotless.

Marjory had told him over their first dinner date Sunday evening that the real Jeff was expected back at work first thing Monday morning and that she had been stressed out on how to handle that situation. Vyllon assured her he would take care of it and had found Jeff's phone first thing after they had returned to the house. He had explained that when he assumed Jeff's form and created what he called a vessel out of what was left of Jeff's consciousness that he had absorbed everything that was Jeff. This included memories, education and character references for how Jeff behaved and reacted to situations as well as people. As a result, it was exceptionally easy for him to access all of Jeff's information and send an email to his business partner stating that he would be taking a leave of absence for the rest of the month. Marjory, unaccustomed to being listened to, had been caught off guard at how easily he had taken care of the situation.

It was now Friday evening, and this was going to be the sixth date she had been on in as many days. The dates had varied from an afternoon spent at the local bookstore with the subsequent and required coffee purchase to casual lunches, followed by trips to museums and even romantic evening dinners for two. Vyllon had taken her out more in the last week than Jeff had in the last couple of years. Jeff had only ever allowed her out in public when he had some sort of business function to attend and needed a trophy to display or to do something mundane like go to the grocery store. Marjory refocused on the task at hand and put the finishing touches on her makeup. Vyllon had advised her to wear something she would be comfortable sitting in for an extend period that was also suitable for a formal evening out. She had no idea what he had planned, but so far; she had not been disappointed in any of his ideas.

Marjory entered her closet and perused her selection of evening gowns. The majority of them were far too revealing for her personal taste, not that she had been the one to pick them out. Her eyes landed on a velvet dress in a green color so dark it was almost black. It had long sleeves that were fitted at the wrist and an empire waist that accentuated her hourglass figure. The neckline buttoned at the hollow of the throat, leaving a mere sliver of her decolletage and the skirt had a slit that came to slightly above the knee. It was the least revealing dress she owned, and she'd never had the opportunity to wear it. Decision made, she slipped into the dress. Because of the cut and fabric, she wasn't able to wear any undergarments under the dress, and as she moved to put her heels on the fabric rubbed against her nipples with the same sensation that her spanked ass had been assaulted by Vyllon's hide. Marjory let out a soft moan and felt her nipples begin to bead with arousal. Vyllon had been overly solicitous of her all week and had not touched her sexually since he had allowed her to orgasm on his tail.

Her body, having been accustomed to being denied pleasure for years, was overly sensitive after Vyllon had eaten her out and fucked her with his tail in the same day. She'd had more orgasms last Saturday than she could remember ever experiencing. Having Vyllon cuddle her all night had been sheer torture; he slept in the nude and hadn't permitted her clothing either. His skin was a tactile assault against her senses, even though he had kept all of his appendages to himself. If he was slowly trying to wear down her resistance, it was working. She could mostly set her arousal aside during the day, but wearing this dress for hours beforehand would prove to be her undoing.

Marjory turned, intending to change out of this dress, when she heard Vyllon enter the room. "You look exquisite," he breathed as he took her in with a look of sheer adoration on his face, his eyes heating with desire as he gazed at her. Marjory felt herself blush at the compliment as she eyed what he was wearing. The formal tuxedo was stretched a bit tight as he had assumed his natural form as he entered the bedroom, but he looked no less handsome in it as Vyllon as he did wearing Jeff's vessel. In all actuality, she was beginning to prefer him in his natural state even though his inhumanness had been jarring at first. She was slowly becoming accustomed to it. Quite frankly, the less she saw of Jeff's face, the better.

"Thank you, this dress is practically new as I haven't ever had the chance to wear it. I take it you approve?" she ended with a question.

"My mate, it is not for me to approve or disapprove but if you need my input. Yes, I very much approve. I will be the envy of every man this evening to have such a beauty as you on my arm. Your loveliness penetrates far deeper than your external beauty, as your aura is one of the most beautiful ones I have beheld in my exceptionally long life. Are you ready to depart? We need to leave within the next fifteen minutes to assure we are not late."

Marjory smiled in abashed pleasure at his response. She had found that he was exceptionally lenient with her, excluding the whole murder thing, and didn't try to dictate to her as she had feared. "I just need to put my shoes and jewelry on, then I'll be ready," she replied. He nodded and turned to leave. "I'll go start the car and warm it for you then," he called over his shoulder as he left. His form morphing back into Jeff as he crossed the threshold of the bedroom. Marjory felt her heart melt at his comment. She hurried as she finished putting her shoes and jewelry on, pausing to grab the overcoat laid across the bed as she strode purposefully out of the bedroom. She had a hot date with her.... well, she wasn't sure what she wanted to call him, but she had a hot date nonetheless and couldn't wait to see what he had in store for this evening.

Chapter Thirteen

Vyllon

Vyllon noted that they arrived at the venue he selected for this evening with plenty of time to spare. His mate was conscientious about being on time to places, while he was less rigid as he was once the being that everyone else waited on and for. Vyllon pulled the car up to the curb, exited and went around to help his little bunny out, nodding his ascent to the valet as he did so. As Marjory situated her gown, her gaze drifted past his shoulder to observe where he had brought her. Her face lit with excitement as she realized they were at the opera house. He smiled at his mate's obvious pleasure. It was quite by accident that he had discovered her love of opera and orchestral music and had only done so after snooping further within her library.

"You brought me to see *The Barber of Seville!*" she

exclaimed with enchanted disbelief, "How in the world did you get tickets, this has been sold out for months since today is the day before Valentine's Day?" she ended in puzzlement. Vyllon cursed under his breath at his shortsightedness. He should have known she would ask. He refused to lie to his mate, even if the truth would mar her delight over this evening's festivities. "I found the tickets hidden in the defiler's memories. He purchased them almost a year ago to attend this function with a plus one," he replied, hoping she would not inquire further.

"I see…so what you aren't saying is that I was not intended as the plus one. You are just trying to spare my feelings and make it more palatable. In my experience, nothing pertaining to Jeff Hempstead was the slightest bit palatable," she remarked, with trace amounts of bitterness clinging to her words. "Whatever, he isn't here. You are, and we aren't going to let that waste of space ruin our night out. It's Valentine's Eve and you've brought me to one of the most romantic venues in the city. Onward, buttercup. There's fuckery to spread!" she ended with a tease, her eyes glittering in mirth at her quip. Vyllon felt the tension coiling within his body slowly loosen. He was grateful that she took what he said in stride, understood what he didn't say, and chose to cast off any negativity in favor of enjoying their evening together. What truly delighted him was her claim that it was *"our"* night out. He extended his arm to her and, to his pleasure, she took his arm, allowing him to escort her up the steps into the opera house. Vyllon made sure he reached the door first and held it open for her to enter. His sharp eyes had perused the lobby through the glass door and ascertained no threat lie within, thus permitting her to enter the room first. Humans and their manners were distinctly backwards from how one should truly enter a room. Vyllon gently removed her black overcoat to reveal the stunning, yet demure, green velvet dress she had selected for her evening wear, allowing one of the staff to take her overcoat. He pocketed the resulting coat ticket for use later in the evening when the performance ended.

"Would you like something to drink before we find our seats? Perhaps hors d'oeuvers? I can see servers making their rounds amongst the guest."

The simple inquiry made her beam up at him in surprised gratitude. It made his black heart ache. Her face reflected her surprise. It was apparent she had never had a man be solicitous of her. Vyllon had been showering her with as much affection and attention as she would permit this past week. He had been permitting her to set the pace of her courting. Excluding punishment, as delicious as it was, he would not touch her without her permission again. He wanted her to love him, not trade one tyrant for another, as she had eloquently, yet explicitly, told him.

"Yes please, that would be wonderful!"

Vyllon lifted his hand and gestured to one of the servers to gain his attention. He gently retrieved a flute of champagne for himself as well as his mate, handing her the glass as she murmured her thanks to him.

"I will flag the next server I see with the hors d'oeuvers, so you can select whatever strikes your fancy, my love."

Vyllon noted how her face softened as his words registered to her as he held her eyes captive in his own, allowing the colors of his true eyes to reflect all the love he possessed within his body. He knew that she was his mate, and he had coveted her above all else on this planet, but he acknowledged to himself that she was right in telling him to court her. His actions at their first meeting, while pleasurable, were not actions that would have endeared him to her for the longevity of what will be an eternal life together. He was as helpless as a child when it came to guarding his heart from her, not that he had even tried. He craved a deeper connection with her. Something more than just a mate connection. Others of his kind had tried to tell him that love would be the ultimate goal of finding his mate, but his arrogance had not allowed him to listen. He had begun to see the true Marjory as she slowly relaxed around him and he earned her trust.

A jarring voice coming from his left interrupted the moment. Vyllon had allowed himself to become enraptured with his mate that he had not paid as close attention to his surrounding as he should. Much to his dismay, one of the females the defiler had been having an affair with was approaching them with hate in her eyes. Externally, she was the epitome of human beauty with a willowy body, baby blue eyes, and sunshine colored hair. However, her aura was tarnished in dark oranges, muddy browns, and slivers of black that were wider in certain places. This human was well on her way to destroying her soul out of vanity, envy and hatefulness. Her aura indicated she relished harming others, and from her purposeful approach, it was clear that she had his little bunny in her sights.

"Jeff, darling! Where on earth have you been? It is quite unlike you to be out of the office for the entire week and when I heard you had taken an extended leave of absence I was caught quite by surprise, especially since we had made previous plans for this weekend," she ended in a falsely sweet, saccharine voice before she continued, "Oh…Marjory, hello. I didn't see you there. How are you?"

"Hello, Terri," his mate deadpanned before turning to address him as if she was informing him of a great secret with a conspiratorial wink. "How awkward this must be for you, Jeff. To have one of your mistresses approach you while you're out with your wife in such a public setting. Oh, Terri. Don't look so shocked. Surely you didn't think I was stupid enough to believe that he was staying late at work to actually work, did you? And yes, I did say ONE of his mistresses because you are not the only one. Oh, I see I struck a nerve with that one. Did you think you were special? How sad for you, I can see that you did. Barbara, that lives down the street from us, is his other mistress. He goes to her when you are out of favor and I am healing from a beating"

Vyllon watched with relish as the female across from blanched white as all the blood drained from her face due to his mate putting the whore in per place. The fact that she thought he was the real Jeff only added to his sadistic glee at watching his mate verbally eviscerate the slattern. Terri's eyes darted to who she thought was Jeff, betrayal written across her features. That she was so gauche as to act the wounded party did nothing but incite his rage. Vyllon glanced around to ensure no one else was paying attention to their little *tet-a-tete* before allowing part of his true form to leak through Jeff's vessel. Betrayal quickly morphed into horror as Terri glimpsed what hid behind his human façade before it faded back to the handsome countenance of Jeff Hempstead.

Vyllon allowed a tendril of his shadow, unnoticeable to the human eye, to slither insidiously across the space between their bodies and pierced it into Terri's chest, hitting her decaying soul with one precise strike. The sensation of something moving inside her body caused the woman to stagger back and grasp her chest, almost clawing at it in panic. He quickly created a shadow bomb within her, sealing it inside the murk of her soul on a delayed timer. She would pay for her transgressions against his mate and for her sins against all the other beings she had wronged. A soul did not get like hers unless a lifetime of evil had been done. The shadow bomb would detonate several hours from now, long enough that neither he nor Marjory could be implicated in her death.

Marjory watched Terri as clinically as one would observe a bug under a microscope. When a militant light came to her eyes, Vyllon knew that she had something else in mind to punish Terri. Marjory turned her body fully to fact him, one hand going to his crotch and gripping his thickening cock as her other hand cupped his jaw and brought his mouth down to hers. The kiss she bestowed upon him was not a gentle thing. Marjory fucked his mouth, the action portraying possession and ownership. Marjory ended the kiss as abruptly as she had started it as she watched Terri gape in horror at them. Marjory offered no further conversation as she observed Terri's frantic motions as the woman backed away from them in terror. Finally, noticing that she had made a spectacle of herself, Terri spun on her heel and hurried away from them as fast as her heels and polite society would allow.

Marjory smiled up at him after the slattern left. "Well, that was fun! I've wanted to do that for years! I also don't want to know what you did to her with that black thing you stuck inside her chest. All I want to know is if she will suffer?" she ended with a viciousness that made his cock throb. Shock tore through him that she had seen his shadow. Apparently, the mate bond between them had strengthened enough, because of their proximity and her trust, that she could see his incorporeal shadows.

"Yes, my love. She will suffer, this I assure you. Shall we take our seats?" he politely inquired, adjusting his cock discreetly while Marjory watched him with a smirk. Vyllon could taste her on his tongue and reveled in it. He didn't care that she had used him to make a point to the slattern. He was ecstatic that she felt safe enough in his regard to do such a thing while he watched with ill-concealed joy as she volun-tarily reached for his arm for the second time this evening and escorted her to their assigned seats like the precious being she was.

Chapter Fourteen

Marjory

The drive home from the opera house was held in companionable silence. Marjory was riding an almost euphoric high because of the evening's activities and the indulgence glances Vyllon kept giving her only stoked that feeling higher. The performance had been better than she had expected it to be and her expectations were fairly high since *The Barber of Seville* was her favorite opera. Not even the altercation with Terri had marred what she considered to be a perfect night out on the town. Actually, the fact that Terri was going to pay for all the pain she had caused made the night that much sweeter. Marjory wondered if she could ask Vyllon to do the same thing to Barbara at the Valentine's Day party the HOA was throwing tomorrow evening. Since removing Jeff from her life, she hadn't planned on attending the party.

However, she was rethinking that decision in light of the discovery that Vyllon would kill whomever had wounded her presently or in the past. She didn't care if that made her a bad person or not. Vyllon had said it was his job to punish those who transgressed against the innocent. Marjory had never hurt anyone. Her sole transgression was that she fell in love with a monster.

Funny that the human she had fallen in love with was a veritable monster and the being beside her appeared to be a monster but treated her like she was precious to him. True, he had been brusque and inappropriate with her, had touched her initially without consent, but since she had spoken up and taken him to task, his behavior had taken a turn for the better. If he'd continued to treat her like a possession, merely his mate, a female that fate had ordained belonged to him, she would have continued to keep him at arm's length emotionally and physically. This evening solidified the fact that she was falling in love with him. Every action he had taken in the last week showcased his growing feelings for her. He had not hidden the fact that he had fallen in love with her earlier this evening, before they were rudely interrupted by fucking Terri. The look he had given her was something Marjory had never been on the receiving end of and it had made her poor, battered heart perk up with hesitant hope. Marjory had never participated in the sexual act with a man that loved her. Losing her virginity to Jeff had been a rough, painful experience that, unfortunately for her, set the tone of her married sex life. Arousal had been growing gradually all night because of the sumptuous feel of her gown slipping and sliding across her body. The subtle graze of claws across her neck as he assisted her into her overcoat prior to their departure had sent streaks of lightning from her nipples straight down to her pussy. The innocent look he had given her didn't fool her at all.

She was pulled from her musings as Vyllon pulled the car into the garage and exited to come open the passenger side door for her, expressing more chivalry in that one gesture than Jeff had in the entirety of their marriage. Marjory extended her hand to him and allowed him to assist her out of the low-slung sports car Jeff had insisted on driving. She murmured her thanks as she made her way into the house, ignoring his deep inhale as she moved past him and into the kitchen. Marjory dropped her evening bag on the kitchen table and walked over to the base of the stairs, kicking her heels off before she ascended them.

Marjory was in her bathrobe, having removed her gown and jewelry, and was going about her bedtime routine by the time Vyllon joined her. Shedding Jeff's vessel as he strode to what was now his walk-in closet. By now, she was accustomed to him joining her in the bedroom and knew that he had been checking to make sure the house was locked for the night. Marjory couldn't see him from where she was standing at the bathroom sink, but the rustle of clothes told her that he was removing the tuxedo. Marjory was arrested by the fact that he had changed forms twice in the same set of clothes, yet they hadn't been destroyed like they had before in the kitchen.

Marjory set her moisturizer down and walked into the bedroom as Vyllon was exiting his closet. "Why didn't the tuxedo rip apart when you shifted forms just now?"

"Ah, noticed that, did you? I've had time to bespell the rest of the clothing with a simple spell that allows me to shift forms without destroying the clothing I am wearing. I had not yet had the opportunity to do so the day I shifted in the kitchen. If you will recall, you caught me somewhat unaware," he remarked sardonically with a lift of his brow. Marjory felt her face heat with embarrassment. She had been trying very hard to forget that she had stabbed him. It filled her with remorse and guilt now to think of her actions.

"It would make sense that beings such as you would need to change forms with ease without destroying clothing, especially if you are undercover," she ended hesitantly. He had not spoken much of what his current duties were, only of his creation and why he was created. "You are correct. There are times that it behooves one of my ilk to have fluidity between our true form and whatever vessel we have selected during an assignment," he further explained as he moved to the bed. Vyllon pulled the covers back and slid into bed with sinuous grace. It almost belied belief that a being as large as he could move so fluidly. Marjory had to remind herself that he was an apex predator and that he would not move according to human standard when he was not enveloped in a vessel.

Marjory felt his ardent gaze on her as she leisurely strolled back into the bathroom to finish getting ready for bed. The sensation of his eyes on her made her flush with pleasure, bringing her waning arousal back to the forefront of her mind. The teasing brush of her gown had stoked her desire all night and his gaze upon her was only inflaming her further. Removing her gown had helped, but the object the gown had reminded her of was front and center. After finishing her nighttime toilette, Marjory exited the bathroom and padded to the bed, shedding her robe and draping it across the chair as she went. The no pajama rule was still very much in effect.

Just as he had every night to date, Vyllon gathered her in his arms and pulled her back against his front as soon as she was settled under the covers. The instant her skin touched his hide, she let out an obscene moan, her fact burning with mortification. Marjory could not be still. Her body began to writhe against him, aching for something more than the teasing feel of his body against hers.

"Do you need relief, little mate? The scent of your wet cunt was quite the distraction all night. Would you tell me why you are so needy?" he whispered in her ear, allowing his tail to come around and gently flick her nipples.

"The dress! The dress I wore this evening is the same texture your skin is, and it teased me for hours!" she gasped out before grabbing his tail and pulling it away from his body. The sound he made was somewhere between a moan and a whimper.

"Your tail is sensitive?"

"Only at the tip and at the base. The rest of it is not as sensitive," he growled out while she massaged the tip of his tail with both of her hands. Marjory rolled over to face him, releasing his tail as she did. Her eyes drifted across his body in wanton perusal from head to toe and back again until her eyes landed on his slit. She had noticed that he had been careful to keep his member hidden within his body every time she had seen him nude.

She reached out her right hand and lightly traced the seam of his slit from top to bottom several times before looking up at him. "What do you have in here hiding away from me?" she whispered seductively, smiling when his breathing picked up and his eyes lit from within, from desire from her boldness.

Chapter Fifteen

Vyllon

Vyllon allowed his painfully aroused cock to fully extrude for the first time within his little bunny's presence without warning. He was solicitous of her, yes, but that did not mean that he wouldn't push her boundaries when he had the chance. She had instigated the touching, and he was going to take as much leeway as she would allow him. He saw her eyes widen as she took in what his body had hidden from her during his wooing. The charcoal color of his cock complimented the pitch-black nature of his hide, but was not the pink-toned thing that a human male would sport. He watched as her eyes widened as she took in the differences between him and what she had known before.

Marjory had jerked her hand away like the touch of his flesh had burned her at the sudden appearance of his member. "Oh…my…I wasn't expecting something like this. Well…to be honest, I had no idea what to expect, but I am glad that you don't have any weird shit going on," she ended on a relieved note, while eyeing his cock in appreciation.

Vyllon chuckled, "My kind were made to be compatible with many species, as our fated mates could belong to any one of a vast variety of beings. It would be best if we were made rather simply as far as genitalia goes."

He was several inches longer and far girthier than the defiler had ever dreamed of being. The overall shape of his cock was the same as a human man, but he was far more substantial and did have one dissimilar trait that she would find out about soon enough. It made pride bloom within him that he could satisfy her far better than anyone ever had or would. She would not know another's touch for the rest of their combined existence.

"May I touch you?"

"Little bunny, my body is yours to do with as you please. You need not ever ask for permission to touch me, but if you need to hear me say it. Yes, you have permission to touch me whenever, and however you so choose." Vyllon ended on a hiss as her soft hands whispered across his throbbing erections. The teasing touches a stark contrast to the extreme need running rampant through his body. He had not told her that not sealing their mating was taking a physical toll on him. He wanted her to choose him and not lie with him out of some misguided sense of guilt over his suffering. When *bogyan* males find their soulmate and touch them for the first time, it caused a pheromone based chemical reaction in the male that sends them into a type of rut. He had been suffering from rut symptoms since he held her that first time while she suffered so terribly.

"I want to know more about what you are and what this mating thing entails," she stated, looking up into his eyes while her hands continued to lightly stroke him.

"*Bogyan,* my kind, only have one soulmate. When beings are born, the souls are split in half and are not complete until both halves find one another. If the souls are born into a mortal body, it can take many reincarnations if the mortal's other half is an immortal, such as is the case with us. Should you choose to finalize our mating bond, the act of sexual congress along with a mating bite will instigate the bond and sew our souls together," he managed to explain in a tortured growl. Her hands were undoing all the control he had forced upon himself. He reached to still her dainty hand with of his far larger ones.

"It would be best if you stopped teasing me. I only have so much control left and I do not think you are ready for me to slip my leash."

Marjory had frozen the second his dark, rough hand had touched hers. "What do you mean?" she asked in confusion.

Vyllon sighed. He would not lie to her even if the truth was not palatable and was the very thing he had been reluctant to tell her from the start. "Males of my ilk go into a rut the first time we touch our mate. I have been in a prolonged rut since I held you while you miscarried your child..." His words had softened and gentled as he delivered the last piece of information to her.

Marjory gaped at him in horror, jerking her hands from his body so abruptly he hissed at the sensation. He sat up in bed, mirroring her actions, his digitigrade legs making it slightly awkward to do so, but he was more worried about his mate than the mild discomfort his body was in.

"That was you? You were the one who held me? The one who comforted me?" she gasped out in disbelief as tears began to roll down her face and her arms came around to cup her sides, before taking a deep breath and continued. "If I'm your mate, why did you leave me with *him?* Why didn't you save me then? I shouldn't have been the one to kill Jeff. YOU SHOULD HAVE KILLED HIM FOR ME!" she screamed at him, her voice so shrill it grated on his sensitive ears, causing him to wince.

"Will you allow me to hold you while I tell you the rest?" he entreated, holding out a hand in supplication. He was shocked when she dove into his arms, her tear-streaked face shoved in the hollow of his throat. Her breathing was choppy as she tried to regain a semblance of calm.

"I may be powerful, but I am not omnipotent. I was sent to the Bahamas on an assignment that another *bogyan* would not have been able to complete. I waited until the bleeding had stopped, cleaned you and put you in bed to rest. Then, despite my personal wants, I left to attend to the task I had been given. If I had known that your husband was the one who had put you in such a state, I never would have left you. I was heartbroken, thinking that my mate, the one I had waited several millennia for, was happily married to a mortal man. I was doomed to watch over you for the rest of your mortal life, while dealing with the fact that my rut had been triggered, and pray that your soul was permitted to be reincarnated and begin searching for you all over again. It was not until the next day when I returned to check on you that I observed your mistreatment at the hands of the defiler. To my dismay, the traffic, then the airport and several thousand miles worth of distance caused me to lose your trail. It's taken me months to locate you. Imagine my surprise when I arrived to see you digging a hole to shove that piece of shit into. I must say, the roses were a brilliant touch, my love," he ended with a soft chuckle as he peered down at her.

His last comment caused her to let out a wet giggle. "Thank you. I appreciate your words of affirmation."

"There is one more thing..." Vyllon began hesitantly, continuing only when she nodded at him to keep going. "...since you're mortal, the bond will...change you. You will still be Marjory; it will take nothing from you, but it will change your body to make it into an immortal like me. Each bonding is different. You could grow horns, or a tail. Your skin could change colors. We won't know until the bond snaps into place and our souls have knitted together. What I can tell you is that you will be able to summon your current form just like I can any vessel I have assimilated over the course of my life, as your current form will be your vessel. The form used to interact with mortals when necessary."

"That…is a lot of information in one bedtime conversation. I honestly don't think I can handle any more revelations. Do you think we could just go to sleep now?" Marjory asked softly, her eyes firmly fixed on his chest. He noted her downcast eyes, dejected body language, and the embarrassed blush staining her cheeks. "I'm so sorry. I didn't mean to be a cock tease, get you hot and bothered, and then change my mind. I swear I didn't do this on purpose. Please tell me you believe me," she ended as her eyes raised to meet his in a beseeching, pleading manner.

Vyllon's ardor had been reduced to a simmer because of his mates' distress, enough that he was able to retract his cock back into his slit. Her tears had caused his rut symptoms to fade to the lowest ebb he had experienced since meeting her. His body instinctively reacting to her emotional state.

"Yes, little one, we can go to sleep now. You've no need to apologize to me. My body is to do with as you so choose. I am your mate. I know you did not instigate physicality with me to utilize my body as a weapon against me. How could you, when you know how it is to be treated thus?" Vyllon crooned as he slid back down the bed, gathering her in his arms as he did so. The shock at his quietly spoken words was written all over her face as she processed what he had said. She visibly calmed after receiving his reassurance that all was well. It wasn't the way he had hoped the evening would end, but he would trade nothing in this world for the trust she had just given him.

Chapter Sixteen

Marjory

The community center the HOA governing this subdivision had built was lit up with a variety of red, pink and white lights as she and Vyllon approached the front door. To Marjory, the decorations looked more like someone had vomited Pepto Bismol all over the building. Barbara Cunningham's work had a signature look, and that look was mediocrity. _They really should have let her do it,_ Marjory thought to herself with glee. She couldn't wait for the HOA board members to see this monstrosity of pink. The décor looked like a high school dance, rather than something an income-based community would boast.

"My love, this building looks as if someone vomited pink all over it. Why does it not look as tasteful as the residence you live in? I have to admit I don't know much about this human holiday, but even I can tell there is a significant difference between this and what you've done," Vyllon asked quietly with faint confusion. That his words echoed her thoughts so closely made her laugh with mirth, a wide smile gracing her face.

"There was a poll in the community for who would be in charge of decoration for this year's Valentine's Day party. Barbara Cunningham, my former husband's other mistress, and I were the two selected. I graciously bowed out of the running after Barbara threw a level ten bitch fit. I knew she wouldn't be able to pull anything off that had a remote not towards elegant romance and wanted to bask in her failure. Fucking bitch that she is won't recover from this for months. If she lives very much longer," she said as she looked over at him in curiosity.

Marjory noticed how his jaw had tightened as she answered his question. It was obvious that he found no amusement that her husband's former mistress, not that she knew she was now a "former mistress," was the one responsible for decorating the party he would be attending this evening. He had been more than mildly intrigued about the human concept of a holiday devoted to nothing but the love to be found between two beings.

After the revelations of last night, Vyllon had suggested they stay home for the day and skip the party. Marjory had agreed with remaining at the house all day, but she had put her foot down about attending the party. Terri was not the only one that had caused her grief, pain, and humiliation.

Barbara had contributed plenty. Every event the HOA hosted, she made it a point to be involved somehow and make sure that everyone knew she was fucking Jeff. Where Terri had been falsely sweet in public, Barbara made no effort to do so. She wanted everyone to know that she was having an affair with the wealthy, handsome Jeff Hempstead and had reveled in rubbing it in Marjory's face every chance she got.

In all honesty, Marjory was looking forward to Vyllon meeting Barbara. Marjory had wondered how he had known what type of person Terri was after one glance and had asked him over breakfast this morning. Vyllon had explained to her that the colors of a person's aura reflected the conditions of the soul housed within the body and how he determined who needed to be removed from the world.

Marjory smiled as Vyllon opened the front door of the community center for her. She noticed how his eyes swept the entire room before she entered. The feeling of being safe was a new concept, but one that she relished. She took in the rest of the decorations as they entered the foyer. The inside of the building didn't look any better than the outside and Marjory could see the judgmental pricks that made up the rest of the community looking around in barely concealed disdain. The room was, quite simply put, tacky when they were accustomed to swanky. It was set up with chairs and tables around the edges, leaving the middle of the room open as a dance floor. Food and drink had been set up along the back wall buffet style so people could come and go as they pleased.

Vyllon escorted her to a table tucked into a corner where

he could see the entire room and both exits. As he pulled out her chair, he murmured "I will go to the refreshment table and get us both something to drink. Do you have any requests?"

"Something light, fruity, bubbly or a combination of all three, please."

The love shining out of his eyes almost took her breath away as he smiled, nodded and turned to walk to the refreshment table. He played the part of Jeff Hempstead well as he smiled, nodded, acknowledged and spoke to people as he walked across the room. Vyllon was flawless in his execution of pretending to be Jeff. She was so bemused with watching him that she didn't notice she had company until the sound of a chair being pulled out from the table interrupted her flagrant admiration of Vyllon. She turned to greet the person next to her only to find Barbara lowering herself into Vyllon's chair, her cornflower blue eyes filled with delighted malice at catching Marjory alone while the muted light of the room made her dishwater blonde hair appear dull.

"Don't you look like the cat who caught the canary? I wonder why you watch him with such love in your eyes when you know he hasn't been faithful to you for a day in your marriage. The fact that you love him makes it that much sweeter for me every time he leaves your bed unsatisfied and comes to mine for true fulfillment. I can give him what he needs in a way you never can," she ended with a prideful sneer, her face twisted in an almost demonic expression.

Shock held Marjory immobile. Love? She didn't love

Vyllon, did she? Marjory took a moment to assess herself as she looked back across the room to see Vyllon frowning as he made his way back to her, a glass in each hand. Marjory realized that even though he wore Jeff's vessel, that she only saw him as he truly was. She didn't see the handsome façade of Jeff Hempstead. Instead, she saw skin black as pitch, towering horns, a naughty tail and rainbow hued eyes that reflected all the love she had ever longed for back at her. It didn't matter what vessel he wore; he was Vyllon; he was *hers*…and she did love him. Vyllon had wormed his way into her wounded heart.

Barabara was many things, but unobservant was not one of them. She mistook Marjory's shock for hurt, one of the few mistakes Barbara had ever made in reading others. Thinking she had wounded Marjory, yet again, she leaned in to whisper to Marjory but was stopped short by a large hand on her shoulder, the nails slightly darker and sharper than they should have been.

Vyllon deftly inserted himself in the space between Marjory and Barbara, forcing the other woman to jump out of her chair or be dumped onto the floor as he shoved the chair away from Marjory with a decisive movement. "Jeff, darling! What on earth are you doing?" Barbara hissed as she straightened her red polka dotted skirt, her eyes flitting about the room to see if anyone had noticed her near mishap.

"Ah, you must be the other one my mate spoke of. Your aura is just as hideous as the female named Terri Smith. I see that name means nothing to you, but it should. You see, you were erroneous in thinking that you were special to Jeff Hempstead. I assure you; you were not. You were his second mistress and the one he called if his first option was not available or it was on a weekend. Especially if he had damaged Marjory to where she was not entertaining enough for his depraved desires," Vyllon growled. The display of pissed off, protective male caused a flush of arousal to spread throughout Marjory's body. She wasn't sure when she started to find his darker side arousing, but it was definitely getting her going now.

"Jeff, I have no idea what you're talking about. I am your one true love. You love me and told me you were going to divorce Marjory so we could be together. She can't satisfy you like I can!" Barbara softly entreated, gazing up at Vyllon with a sickening amount of freakish devotion shining in her eyes. She extended one of her hands, as if she was going to stroke his chest, but was stopped by a deep growl. A growl that a human man was not capable of making.

"Female, you dare to try to touch me! I can see by your aura that you are not capable of true, abiding love. Your life choices have damaged your soul and polluted it. You are a vicious, grasping harpy that only delights in taking what she wants from those that she envies. As the first *bogyan* it is my duty, but as my little bunny's mate, it is my privilege to rid the world of a being like you. I believe it is time for you to remove yourself from our presence, as you have overstayed the welcome that wasn't extended to you.," he ended with a vicious sneer. Marjory noticed a thin, almost translucent tendril extending from Vyllon's chest and entered the area between Barabara's over inflated fake boobs. It was where her heart, if she actually had one, would be. Marjory watched Barbara flinch at the sensation of movement in her chest, her reaction almost identical to Terri's as she raised a hand to grasp at her chest. It would seem that Vyllon had allowed both women to feel what he was doing instead of being subtle about it. Barbara took a decisive step away from Vyllon in confusion at the words that were being cast at her by, who, she thought, an angry, disdainful Jeff Hempstead. Her face was an artful mask displaying what she thought Jeff wanted to see. However, that was quickly morphing into something reminiscent of a vindictive, wronged woman. She was the one fucking a married man. She had no right to be offended at being put in her place. As Barbara opened her mouth to fire off some sort of cutting remark, Marjory stepped into the space left vacant when Barbara had staggered back from Vyllon.

Vyllon dragged her back to his front as his arms came around her in a proprietary hold. The abrupt move shocked the other woman so much she was rendered speechless. Jeff had never permitted Marjory to be familiar with him in public, let alone to be the one to instigate some sort of physical affection. Marjory allowed her weight to rest against Vyllon and subtly ground her ass into his groin, deliberately trying to arouse him. If she was hot and bothered, then he needed to be as well.

"You may leave now, Barbara. As you can see, you are

clearly the third wheel and aren't wanted. I would suggest you do as my husband says and leave while you still have a modicum of dignity intact, and I suggest closing your mouth. You look like a fish that's been tossed on the bank, gasping for water. It's rather unattractive," Marjory tittered in a coquettish fashion, batting her eyelashes at Barbara to add insult to injury. It was nothing the bitch hadn't earned. With one final huff, she spun on her heel and left.

As soon as she had departed their company, Vyllon grabbed her hips in both hands, pulling her ass tighter to him, hissing at the added pressure on his groin.

"Would you like to dance, my love?"

Marjory glanced at the dancefloor full of couples swaying to cheesy love songs, then turned her head to look back at him over her shoulder. "No, I think you need to take me home and make me your mate."

The look of incandescent joy that came across his face was something she had never seen on Jeff Hempstead before. It made a handsome visage into something breathtaking, but it couldn't compare to what she knew he truly looked like. That form far surpassed any other version of male beauty she'd ever seen. Vyllon didn't hesitate as he scooped her up into his arms bridal style and carried her all the way back to their house.

Chapter Seventeen

Marjory

Marjory watched as Vyllon's true form gradually appeared as he carried her into their bedroom. His body lengthened and stretched around her, the sensation of his velvet hide, teasing her skin in a seductive caress. She could tell that he was trying not to frighten her with the depth of his need. She now understood that he had suffered while trying to find her and had decided to suffer endlessly rather than potentially upset her marriage. The sheer selflessness he exhibited had probably been the final nail in her emotional coffin. If he had been maddened with need from his rut, his initial actions, while unacceptable, were now explained and understood.

Marjory smiled up at him as he gently laid her on their bed, as she reached up, grabbed his horns in a firm hold and dragged his face down to hers while holding his rainbow eyes firmly with her icy ones. "I had an epiphany earlier while whore number 2 was attempting to speak to me."

"And what would that be, my love?" he softly asked.

"I love you, Vyllon. You've managed to sneak your way into my tattered heart and entrench yourself there. I didn't think it was possible for me to love anyone, not after my last experience with love. The universe, or whoever makes these decisions, knew that I needed you to help me stitch myself back together. I know I am not weak. I never would have survived Jeff if I was, so I have no issue admitting that I need you in my life. What I can tell you is that I don't want you to hold back, thinking that I can't handle you. You told me that your rut has been a problem since last summer. I am giving you full carte blanche to let it loose and show me what I've been missing my entire life."

The last word had barely left her mouth when she watched his control snap as his baser nature took over his conscious mind. He loomed over her on the bed, his massive body blocking her from being able to escape. Not that she wanted to, but it had to be an instinctive act. Marjory watched as his claws emerged from his fingertips and tore her clothes from her body in a vicious display of dominance. A deep, rumbling growl was emanating from his chest that was making her pussy weep with need. She made no move to stop him as he used the tattered remains of her clothes to tie her hands to the slatted headboard above her head.

Vyllon paused for a moment, gazing down at her luscious

bare body that was completely at his mercy, as if he didn't know where to start. Marjory giggled a bit at his indecisiveness and shimmied her heavy breast at him. Her nipples had been aching since he laid her down and needed his mouth's attention. His gaze snapped to her breast, following the swaying motion as if he was hypnotized.

Marjory let out an obscene moan the moment his mouth closed around her left nipple, his sharp teeth scraping gently over the hardened tip before he started sucking at her in a hard, rhythmic fashion as he tweaked and pinched her other nipple. His free hand suddenly appeared at her throat and collared her there, holding her in place as he took his time learning her body. The sensation of something touching her pussy caused Marjory to whine with need. He moved his knees between her legs, forcing them to open wide to accommodate his bulk and allow his tail easier access to her pussy as he moved his mouth to her other nipple, lavishing attention on the neglected, aching flesh. The textured tip of his tail flicked across her clit, causing Marjory to lift her hips, as she tried to chase the sensation his tail kept teasing her with. A rough chuckle caught her attention as Vyllon lifted his head from her breast.

"Don't worry, little mate, I will satisfy you soon enough. You will submit to me in all ways before the night is through," he darkly promised.

"Well, I don't want to wait while you dick around, hurry up and fuck me or I will find someone else who will!" she snapped at him in frustration, tired of his teasing and honed in on the one thing that would piss him off enough to get him to do what she wanted.

The snarl that came from him should have scared her, but it did nothing but make her hotter for him. Her pussy gushed as her body registered the threat he had just issued. He gave her no warning before his enormous cock was notched at her opening and he surged into her in one smooth thrust. The sheer size of him overwhelmed her as he began pumping into her body without mercy. Continuous snarls came from his lips as he loomed over her. He angled his head and began to devour her mouth, his tongue ravishing her the same way his cock was. His cock shouldn't have fit without thorough preparation, but her threat goaded him to the point he took her roughly instead of gently taking his time. He kept her pinned to the bed by her throat with one of his large, claw tipped hands as he lifted her hips with the other, altering the angle at which his cock hit her g-spot as his hips hammered against hers. The new angle allowed his tail enough space to reach around her body to brush against where their bodies were joined, gathering slick on its rough, bumpy surface that when he pressed his tail to her ass, the tip penetrated her with ease. Vyllon wrenched his mouth from hers when he felt her tense.

"You will deny me nothing, I will claim every orifice on this delectable body, now relax and let me have that sweet ass," he demanded while pressing his tail deeper into her ass with steady pressure, not waiting for her to heed his order. Marjory was almost past coherent thought as his heavy cock hammered her pussy as his tail fully entered her ass and began and alternating rhythm with his cock. The feeling of being double penetrated was overwhelming. She felt the pressure in her lower abdomen begin to build as her body was preparing to climax. The tingling of an impending orgasm had just begun when Vyllon stopped moving completely. Marjory opened her eyes to glare up at him in frustrated disbelief.

"What the fuck, Vyllon?" she screeched, her body on the precipice of completion. Marjory watched him as her frustration grew, her body writhing on his cock and tail trying to force enough sensation to get her off. The pressure at her throat intensified as he dropped her hips to the bed, pinning her in place with the weight of his body. This forced her body into stillness, but added to the sensation of his hide rubbing against her entire body. Marjory whined at him, her tone pleading with him to let her cum. He said nothing and waited for her body to calm, her orgasm slowly fading away. Marjory wasn't sure how he knew, but as soon as the urge to cum left her, he began slamming his hips into hers and twisting his tail buried in her ass viciously, building her body to a fever pitch before stopping a second time. The need to cum was so intense Marjory was in tears as she begged, pleaded, threatened and cajoled Vyllon to let her come.

"Who do you belong to, little bunny? Who owns this body? Who is your mate?" his deep voice questioned her, watching as tears rolled down her face. His tongue reached out and licked the salty tracks from her cheeks. "Answer me and I will give you what you need."

"I belong to you, you fucking edging asshole," Marjory yelled up at him, glaring at him with unfulfilled need in her eyes.

He bared his teeth in a facsimile of a smile at her words before he picked up a brutal, punishing pace, slamming his body into hers ruthlessly. He slid his hand up her throat to her jaw, turning her head to the side, leaving her throat exposed to his gaze. Her eyes slid closed as he manipulated her body, building her climax for a third time. The need to cum was so great it almost hurt. She was almost mindless with need by this point, her body screaming for relief. The telltale tingling in her lower abdomen appeared again as opened her eyes and locked gazes with him as she screamed. "Oh, Vyllon, please, love, don't stop this time! I'm yours. Your mate. I belong to you, but you fucking well belong to me too!"

Stars exploded behind her eyes as she came; the pressure building finally snapped as bliss encompassed her entire body. The pinch of pain where her neck and shoulder met was nothing compared to the overwhelming pleasure surging through her entire body. She could feel Vyllon's cock surging into her as he chased his completion as well. He kept fucking in her through her first orgasm, not slowing and showing her no mercy as his teeth remained embedded in her flesh. Marjory felt a second orgasm hit her, just as powerful as the first, as his hips continued to slap against hers. The sensation of his cock getting thicker took her by surprise. The motion of his hips became shorter and jerkier as his cock thickened. His thumb appeared on her clit and began to massage it vigorously. Her exhausted body burst as he forced a third orgasm from her, wrenching his mouth from her shoulder as he roared out his completion. His cock was embedded in her. The knot he'd failed to mention lodged him deep within in her body as she felt his seed jetson deep into her body. Each ejaculation against her womb caused her body to twitch and moan at the sensation.

Marjory became aware of the feeling of heat emanating from where he bit her and her womb, where he had deposited his seed deep within her body. The heat wasn't painful; it was like warming your hands in front of a fire after being out in the cold. The heat swept through her entire body, getting hotter and hotter. She looked up at Vyllon in alarm. Something wasn't right.

"Shhhh, little love, let it happen," he reassured her.

The heat pulsed and pooled in her pussy, causing her ardor to flame back to a fever pitch. Vyllon picked her up and walked over to the wall, pinning her against the hard surface, moving his hands to cup her ass in support as he began to fuck her ruthlessly, his knot restricting him to short strokes that forced his hide to grind into her overstimulated clit. The burn of the mate bond drove them both higher and higher until they were both panting with need for the other. The hot sensation of their souls being branded together was the ultimate culmination and caused them to peak simultaneously. Vyllon managed to stumble back over to the bed, exhaustion lining his face as he laid down with Marjory impaled atop him, his cock still locked deep in her pussy.

Marjory looked up at him with bleary eyes and smiled. "Well, that was definitely worth the wait."

She fell asleep to the sound of his deep, rumbling laugh, missing his softly spoken words as she did.

"I would wait for you for eternity."

Epilogue

Marjory

Some might think that attending the funerals of your murdered husband's mistresses was tacky, but Marjory Hempstead didn't give a fuck. Sure, she and Vyllon had received some incredulous looks, but Marjory still didn't give a fuck. If Marjory had her way, she would have danced on both bitches' corpses. They had just returned home from Barbara's funeral and had attended Terri's yesterday. Both funerals had taken place the week after her bonding with Vyllon.

Vyllon, utilizing Jeff's memories, had slid into Jeff's life seamlessly. He went to work during the day, playing the part perfectly. Vyllon didn't really answer to anyone unless he transgressed against an innocent. He had told her he would take as much time off from his *bogyan* duties as she needed in order to acclimate to her new life. Her mind wandered as she thought about how much her life had changed recently. Her body going through the motions of removing her funeral attire. Her sex drive had increased tremendously after finalizing her mating with Vyllon, but that wasn't the only thing that had changed. Her eyes had remained icy blue and her hair was still white blonde, but her skin tone wasn't milk pale anymore. She was speckled with silver and gold sparkles across her entire body. She was the brightness to his darkness. The contrast of their bodies next to one another was beautiful. Vyllon had been struck speechless the first time he saw her new form. He had told her that her skin was just as bright as her aura. Her inner light had pushed out until it decorated her skin. Several days after their mating night, he had called a healer to come check her over. He wanted to make sure everything was as it should be since her body had basically evolved from mortal to immortal to become compatible with him. Marjory had been shocked to learn that she was capable of having children. The heat that had pooled in her pelvis causing her surge of arousal had also healed the damage caused by her miscarriage. She'd told Vyllon that she wanted children with him but wasn't ready to try again anytime soon.

Marjory's eyes lit as her mate walked into the bedroom, shivering as her need for him began to build. She smiled, sharp teeth flashing, as his tail twined with hers, tugging on it seductively. A large hand grabbed one of her delicate, arcing horns to force her head back, baring her throat to his hot tongue.

"Are you happy, my love?" he gently inquired as he nibbled her mating mark.

"Everything I dreamed of has come true and you will never know how glad I am that you are not Jeff." she snarked.

Marjory beamed at him as he threw his head back, laughter booming out of him at her quip.

She couldn't wait to spend eternity with the love of her life.

The end.

Dear Reader

Dear Reader:

Thank you for taking the time to read this book! Vyllon and Marjory was a silly story that I spun at my day job to a coworker while humming along to Kelsea Ballerini's song *If You Go Down (I'm Going Down Too)*. Said coworker looked over at me and said "That needs to be a book!" Being an author has been a lifelong dream of mine so I decided to take the leap with my debut novella about Vyllon and Marjory. I hope you'll consider leaving me a review of what you thought about **King of Death**. It doesn't have to be long; a short sentence will do! Reviews help authors find new readers, and help others find new books!

Upcoming Releases!

I am currently working on a Romantasy Novel about a grouchy dragon warrior and his fated mate…that runs away from him the first time she sees him. Look for this release later in 2024!

About the Author

Jewel Shipley is a new author, debuting her novella about the Boogeyman finding love. She is all about the sunshine/grump trope and the anti-hero finding his one true love. She has a soft spot for the underdog and happily ever after endings.

Sign up for my newsletter and enter the world of Jewel's JewelTones:

http://eepurl.com/iI28mE

 facebook.com/jewel.shipley.2024

 bookbub.com/profile/3192140199

www.ingramcontent.com/pod-product-compliance
Lightning Source LLC
Chambersburg PA
CBHW061434160726

47995CB00003B/884